A Fool FOR YOU

A FOOLPROOF LOVE NOVEL

KATEE ROBERT

Entangled Publishing, LLC
2614 South Timberline Road
Suite 109
Fort Collins, CO 80525
Visit our website at www.entangledpublishing.com.

Brazen is an imprint of Entangled Publishing, LLC. For more information on our titles, visit www.brazenbooks.com.

Edited by Heather Howland
Cover design by Heather Howland
Cover photo by Lindee Robinson Photography, featuring Travis Bendall and Daria Rottenberk

Manufactured in the United States of America

First Edition October 2016

ENTANGLED
BRAZEN

Dear Reader,

The Foolproof Love series is so incredibly close to my heart for many different reasons. It was the first category romance series I ever contracted, and it went through many incarnations before finding its way into your hands. It's also filled to the brim with some of my favorite characters and stories that I've written to date. The series wraps up with Daniel and Hope's story. It's been a long time in coming, and they've both had quite the winding journey through endlessly rocky roads.

For the heroes in this series, the car wreck that happened thirteen years previous was the turning point in a lot of ways. It spurred Adam into leaving Devil's Falls for all but the shortest visits. It was the shot of reality Quinn needed to leave his family's plans behind him for good. But for Daniel, it was the one event he can't get past. He's been stuck in place ever since, and he needs some meddling to get him back to reality. And we all know that meddling is what the Rodriguez family does best.

We met Hope briefly in the last book, and words cannot encompass my love for her. She's a fighter and a survivor and she's probably more well-adjusted than most of the heroines I write... Except when it comes to her blast from the past. There's no telling what will happen when two people who loved so intensely and fell apart so spectacularly come together again.

So settle in, lovely readers. I hope you enjoy reading this story as much as I enjoyed writing it.

This one's for you.

To my readers.

Chapter One

Hope Moore held her breath as she passed the sign declaring WELCOME TO DEVIL'S FALLS. She hadn't crossed the town boundary in thirteen years, not since she sat next to an open grave as they lowered her brother into the ground. Not since she turned her back on her entire life here, whisked away by her parents to the best medical facilities Texas had to offer.

She touched her knee. She'd never cheered again, never run track, never done any of the things she'd had planned when she was eighteen and had graduated high school with stars in her eyes.

Stars in her eyes, and love in her heart.

Neither had lasted past that car crash.

Oh, it had taken the love a lot longer to die than it had her knee, but Daniel Rodriguez made sure she knew where she stood with him.

She caught herself taking her foot off the gas and picked up speed again. There was no telling if she'd see him while she was here, but it couldn't matter. She'd moved past what happened that night, moved past the disappointment that she'd almost let sour everything else about her life. It might not have happened like she planned, but she'd made the best of her college experience, and she'd gone on to create a successful little niche for herself, helping people and institutions with too much money on their hands create trusts and scholarships for those in need.

And now Hope was back in town to finally do that in her brother's memory.

She pulled onto Main Street, heading for the only lodgings someone out of town with no relatives to stay with would consider—Sara Jane's B&B. It was a nice little place, but Sara Jane was nosy to a criminal degree and gossiped more than anyone Hope had ever come across. The second she checked in and went up to her room, everyone with a phone would be getting a call letting them know that she was back in town.

It wasn't that it was a secret, but she couldn't help but feel that she'd always be John Moore's little sister, the one who survived when her older brother—her better in a lot of ways—didn't. She *knew* that was her own insecurity. She'd had too many years of therapy to believe anything else, except in her darkest heart of hearts, the place she didn't let see the light any more than strictly necessary.

But it was hard to ignore that little voice when driving through Devil's Falls. No, not through. *To.* This was her destination.

Her parents hadn't been too thrilled about her coming back, even for a limited time, but even they couldn't deny that this scholarship she was here to set up was a good thing—the right way to honor John. He'd been in the middle of a full ride at the University of Texas when he was killed, and it made sense to set it up to allow other kids the opportunity he'd never be able to realize.

She pressed a hand to her chest and pulled into the nearest parking spot against the curb. *God, even after all this time, it still hurts.* Most days it didn't. He'd been gone long enough that she'd processed her grief as much as one person could process grief, and she was able to focus on the good memories.

Most days.

Her eyes focused on the sign she'd been staring blindly at, and she frowned. CUPS AND KITTENS. That was new. In a town as mired in the past as Devil's Falls, change was something of a novelty. Or maybe she was biased in a negative way, because the only thing this town held for her was memories. Some bad, mostly good, all dust now.

Pathetically grateful for something external to focus on, she climbed out of her car and looked at the cheery window painting depicting kittens frolicking in between flowers.

The B&B could wait a little while longer. Her meeting with the town board wasn't until tomorrow, so there was no reason she couldn't do a little poking around in the meantime. Thirteen years was a long time. If anyone had asked her, she would have joked that she hadn't expected anything about Devil's Falls to change while she was gone.

Apparently she'd been wrong.

She pushed through the door and froze in the face of a pair of cats staring at her from their perch on a table overlooking the big window in the front. The sight surprised a laugh out of her. "Cups and Kittens, indeed."

"In the most literal sense."

She glanced over at the woman behind the counter, a third cat lounging near the register. Familiarity rolled over Hope. "Jules Rodriguez." Daniel's little cousin. Not so little anymore. Last time she'd seen Jules, the girl had been lanky to an almost awkward degree and had braces with bright green bands. She'd grown up pretty, and there was more of Daniel about her now than there had been when she was a kid.

Or maybe I'm just back in Devil's Falls and seeing Daniel

wherever I look.

Jules's dark eyes cleared. "Hope? What are you doing back in town?" She hesitated. "I don't suppose you're here to sweep my brooding cousin off his feet and shove him back into real life?"

Her mind tripped over itself trying to keep up with the other woman's verbal gymnastics. Jules had always been like that, now that she thought about it—a bright and bubbly steamroller. She tried to weed her way through what the woman had just said, but there was only one thing she could focus on. Daniel. Always Daniel. "What do you mean, back into real life?"

"Well, you know."

No, she really didn't. She studied Jules's face, the way she wouldn't quite meet her eyes. "Is he okay?" She hadn't missed the way Quinn Baldwyn had frozen up when she'd asked that same question a few weeks ago at his sister's wedding, and worry had been simmering in the back of her mind ever since, no matter how many times she told herself it wasn't any of her business. Daniel was a grown man, and he had always been more than capable of taking care of himself—and everyone else around him. Things changed, but she couldn't see *that* changing.

Jules shifted, her hand darting out to pet the calico on the counter and then darting away when the cat swiped at her. "Define okay."

It was none of her business. It stopped being her business a very long time ago.

But that didn't stop her from clearing her throat and asking, "Is he…is he married?" *Did he build the house we always talked about and have those two wild boys and one sweet girl? Does he bring his wife waffles for breakfast in bed on the weekends?*

Oh my God, stop.

But Jules was already shaking her head, her mouth turning down. "Nope. No wife, no kids, no serious relationship in, well, thirteen years."

Hope blinked. "You're joking."

"I wish I was." A calculating look came into her eyes, but then she shook herself and it was all guileless enthusiasm. "What are you doing for dinner?" She rushed on without waiting for a response. "We're having a little thing with Quinn and my friend Aubry, and, well, I kind of went and married Adam Meyers."

Some things really do *change.* She remembered Adam, the wild-eyed boy who'd grown into a wild-eyed man, better than she remembered Jules. No one had expected him to come back to Devil's Falls after he blew out of town that last time, let alone to settle here and…get married. "Wow. What's Daniel have to say about that?"

"He was best man at our wedding." Jules laughed. "Though he was pretty furious at the beginning. Here, sit down. You look like you could use a coffee, and I'll tell you the story since we're generally pretty dead Thursday nights. Then I'll close up and we can go to dinner. The boys will love to see you. Quinn was just talking about you the other day."

Hope wasn't sure she actually agreed to any of it, but the next thing she knew, she was drinking coffee while a cat curled up in her lap and listening to Jules's wild tale about a fake relationship that turned into a real relationship. Somehow in the middle of that, she was bundled up into Jules's truck, and by then it was too late to change her mind.

She settled into her seat, consoling herself with the fact that Jules had very specifically *not* mentioned Daniel's name. There was no reason to think he'd be there, but it *would* be nice to reconnect with some of her old friends. As much as it had hurt when things went south with Daniel, knowing that she'd lost Quinn and Adam, too, had just been salt in the wound. She'd chased them around since she could toddle after her big brother and his friends, and they'd turned into true friends over the years. She understood why they hadn't reached out, but she wasn't going to turn down a chance to catch up with them.

It would probably be the only nice thing about being back in Devil's Falls.

• • •

"Not interested."

"You haven't even heard what I'm asking."

"Don't need to." Daniel Rodriguez leaned down and unbuckled Rita's saddle and hefted it off the horse's back. They'd had a good run today, the hot sun making it impossible to think too hard about anything other than whether a human being could roast alive in Texas in August. He hadn't yet, so that put the odds ever so slightly in his favor.

All he wanted was to finish here and head back to his place for a cold shower and an even colder beer.

It would just fucking figure that the universe had other ideas. He glanced up, but Aubry Kaiser hadn't moved. In fact, with her arms crossed over her chest and her chin up, all signs pointed to this adding up to an argument he couldn't possibly win.

Damn it.

"No."

She frowned harder. "It's your birthday. You can't just sit at home by yourself."

"Since it's my birthday, this is the one day a year I should be able to do *exactly* that with no one bitching at me." He regretted the harsh words almost as soon as they were out of his mouth, but Aubry wasn't like his little cousin. She was meaner than a rattler and twice as likely to bite.

She narrowed her amber eyes at him. "Your cousin misses you."

That explained why she was out here when he knew for a fact she thought horses were akin to goats—as in, the devil's own creatures. Hell, she was giving poor Rita a suspicious look even while guilt-tripping him using the one person in his life he couldn't say no to.

Which doesn't explain why Jules herself isn't here.

"She sees me on a regular basis."

"This is your birthday." Aubry sighed and rolled her eyes, looking put-upon. "Look, it goes like this—Jules has worked really hard to put together a surprise birthday party for you, and if you don't show up to be surprised, she's going to be crushed."

He stared. "I don't want a surprise birthday party." The fact that it was no longer a surprise said a whole lot about Aubry's priorities, and he couldn't blame her for that.

"Look at my face. This is the face of a woman who doesn't give two fucks what you care about. What *I* care about is Jules, and that means you're going to go shower off the smell of that animal and show up at their house in an hour, right on time." She paused, her brows slanting down in an expression that was downright forbidding. "You helped me out not too long ago, so I'm going to do you a solid and give you the lowdown. Ready?"

Fuck, no. "Sure."

"Jules is worried about you. Really worried. If you don't show up tonight, she's going to take that as a sign to go forward with plan B."

He knew he was going to regret it, but he still asked, "What's plan B?"

Aubry gave a tight smile. "A full-scale intervention with everyone in your life, including your parents. The kind where they sit you down in a circle and each speak their mind in the most uncomfortable way possible until you're ready to beg the ground to swallow you whole." Her smile dimmed. "She's worried about you, Daniel."

Everyone seemed worried about him, though they usually did him the courtesy of at least trying to hide the looks exchanged when they thought he wasn't looking. The whispered conversations with his various cousins and his parents. The never-ending work that was only there because they were throwing him a goddamn bone. It didn't seem to matter that he hadn't done anything requiring an intervention. He'd just stopped enjoying the company of people, mostly because he was such shitty company these days. But try telling that to the family, and they acted like he had just confessed to being an ax murderer.

At least Jules had mostly stayed out of it. Up until today.

He grabbed the curry brush and went over Rita's back. Aubry was right. Showing up to a party he didn't want on a day he sure as fuck didn't feel like celebrating was vastly preferable to the alternative. "Explain to me what the plan is."

She gave a grin that did nothing to reassure him. "Dinner and drinks. It'll be nice. Adam and Quinn miss you."

"I see those assholes every day." Kind of hard not to when they worked the ranch alongside him. It felt right to have Adam back, to have Quinn there, but at the same time it was a constant reminder that they were a man short.

And it was his fault.

"It's different and you know it," Aubry continued, obviously enjoying how miserable he was. She'd always been a mean one, which never failed to amuse him because Jules was her polar opposite — as bright and happy as a spring day. Rita shifted in her stall, and Aubry went even paler than she was normally. "Dinner starts at six. Don't be late." Then she was gone, moving at a clip fast enough that a less cautious man than Daniel would call it running.

He waited a good five minutes before he followed, hauling the saddle into the tack room and sorting out the bridle. He didn't begrudge Quinn his happiness—or Adam, for that matter—but sometimes it sure as fuck was hard to be around them and their women. The fact that one of those women was his little cousin barely entered into it.

He headed for his truck and took the pitted dirt road leading around the edge of his parents' property to the little house he'd built a few years ago. It wasn't anything fancy, but it got the job done, and it was far enough outside town that most people thought twice before stopping by unannounced.

Most people not including his family.

The shower did nothing to ward off the feeling of pending doom. It wasn't that he didn't like Jules or Adam or Quinn or whoever the fuck else was going to be at this damn party, but he wasn't in the partying sort of mood. Truth be told, he hadn't been in that mood for over a decade. It was almost enough to make him call the whole thing off, but the knowledge that Jules would have no problem bringing the party to him got him moving again. Not to mention the potential *intervention* he needed like he needed a hole in the head.

At least if he went there, he could hang out for the appropriate amount of time, make his excuses, and slip out while everyone else was occupied. Two hours, tops.

Feeling significantly better, he pulled on a pair of his favorite old jeans and a T-shirt and grabbed his keys. It struck him as he walked out the door that he was thirty-fucking-four years old. *How the hell did that happen?* He shook his head. He knew damn well how that happened. One day turned into a week, a month, a year, a decade. All while he kept on keeping, the world changing around him, but never changing enough.

He glanced at his watch. "Two hours starts when I get there."

Chapter Two

Daniel figured out the entire party was a mistake ten minutes in, which was right around the time Adam and Quinn walked in the back door with a motherfucking *puppy*. He shook his head, backing away. "No."

"It was this or that little hellion Mr. Winkles."

Thinking of that asshole cat who currently resided in Jules's cat café, Daniel cringed. Then he made the mistake of looking at the dog in Quinn's arms. The big man dwarfed the tiny pup, which had to contribute to how cute the little fella was. He was a border collie and had big blue eyes and a patchy fur coloring that was black, brown, and white. His left ear flopped down, and if he wasn't the cutest little thing...

Goddamn it.

"I don't want a dog." His heart wasn't really in the protest, though, so when Quinn offered the pup, Daniel took him. The pup immediately scrambled up against him and licked his chin. "Though he's cute."

"She."

That startled a laugh out of him. "The last thing I need in

my life is a woman, and both you assholes damn well know it."

Adam got a funny look on his face, one Daniel would have called guilty. "Yeah, well, about that. Brace yourself."

He didn't get a chance to ask what the fuck his friend meant by that because the front door opened behind him and Jules's voice rang out, "Honey, I'm home."

"Hey, sugar." But Adam's voice wasn't quite right, and he was looking over Daniel's right shoulder when Jules was clearly behind his left.

For one eternal moment, Daniel considered shouldering past his friends and walking out the back door. Whatever put *that* look on Quinn and Adam's faces wasn't something he wanted to deal with. They almost looked like they'd seen a ghost.

But his dad hadn't raised a coward, so he took a deep breath and turned around.

And froze.

She looks the same.

He blinked, but Hope Moore didn't disappear. She just stood in the doorway, her blond hair pulled back in an effortless ponytail, her face older than when he'd last seen her but more beautiful for the years written across it. Her body had filled out, her hips and breasts curvier than they'd been at eighteen. She didn't look like a girl anymore. No, Hope was full woman.

And then, because he couldn't help it, his gaze dropped to her left leg. Her skirt was too long to see the scar he knew must wind down her leg, the scar *he'd* put there. Knee replacements weren't pretty, and her bones had already been mangled by the time she made it to the hospital, her entire future ruined in the space of a single heartbeat.

Because of him.

She flinched, which was answer enough. He hadn't

imagined it, and the handful of surgeries, the months and months of recovery, the loss of her cross-country scholarship, all of it, had really happened to her. *What's the ability to run compared to a brother? You fucked everything beyond recognition.* He dragged his attention back to her face, determined not to look at her leg again. He'd been the one responsible—the least he could do was avoid making her feel uncomfortable.

She recovered quickly, offering him a small, sad smile. "Hey, Daniel."

"What are you doing here?" It came out too harsh, but he didn't take the words back. Thirteen goddamn years and she chose *today* to show up in Devil's Falls? It wasn't a coincidence, and he had a feeling he knew whom to blame. He spun and pointed a finger at Quinn, keeping his hold on the pup gentle despite his growing anger. "You. What the fuck did you do?" He knew Quinn had seen Hope last month at his sister's wedding, which meant he'd opened his idiot mouth and said something to bring her home.

You should be thanking him.

Fuck that. She doesn't want to be here. If she did, she would have come back before now.

Quinn held up his hands. "Don't look at me. This isn't my style, and you know it."

He had a point. Both his friends were more direct than to pull some shit like this. Jules, though… Daniel turned to glare at her. "This is out of line—even for you."

For her part, she didn't look the least bit repentant. She propped her hands on her hips. "Fun fact—Hope is a grown woman who's more than capable of making her own decisions. She wandered into my shop and I was polite enough to invite her along. I didn't kidnap her." She motioned at Hope. "Tell him I didn't kidnap you."

Despite everything going on around them, Hope burst

out laughing. Daniel's chest gave a lurch. Fuck, the woman's laugh could still do a number on him. All these years later, she should have sounded different from the innocent girl he'd been head over heels in love with. Too much had changed for her to still love life as much as she had back then.

Hadn't it?

Hope shook her head, still laughing. "I can attest that I drove into town of my own free will. I take no responsibility for what happened after that cup of coffee. Jules is a hard woman to say no to." She pinned him in place with those dark eyes. "Happy birthday, Danny."

No one had called him that in…well, hell, in thirteen years. Hearing it on her lips nearly had him crossing the room to her and seeing what else was the same. Common sense stopped him cold. Whatever had brought Hope back into town, she wasn't here for him. There was no forgiving what he'd done, and he'd be worse than a fool to forget that.

It took everything he had to dredge up a halfhearted smile. "Thanks."

The pup wiggled in his arms and gave a mournful whine. He took the excuse to get the hell out of there. "Be back in a bit." He had no intention of coming back. Forget worrying about being cowardly—the last thing he wanted to do was stand in a room with Hope Moore and make small talk. As much as the sight of her was like a rain after a long drought, there was too much shit between them.

She should have stayed away. Whatever brought her back here, it could have been avoided.

He set the pup down in the yard and crouched next to her, watching her run back and forth, still in the awkward stage where her paws seemed too big for her body. She really was a cutie. She was also going to need a name. "How about Ollie?"

"I like it."

He turned to find Hope standing behind him. Again.

"You sure move quiet when you want to." Especially for a woman with a bum leg. Not that he could say as much without sounding like a jackass.

"You mean since I had my knee replaced." Of course she knew what he meant anyway. Apparently damn near reading his mind was one annoying habit she hadn't outgrown.

"I didn't say that."

"You didn't have to." She leveraged herself down next to him, the move not quiet as smooth as it'd been when she was eighteen.

Daniel almost cursed. He had to stop doing that. Comparing her now to how she was then wasn't fair to either of them. It was another lifetime completely, and thinking about it was just fucking depressing. "Hope—"

"Are you seeing anyone?"

"No."

"Why not?"

He was so surprised by the question that he answered honestly, "Why the fuck would I bother?"

"Oh, I don't know, because you don't want to be a creepy old man who lives in the middle of nowhere and has to run off silly high school kids with his shotgun because they tell ghost stories about him?"

He looked at her, half sure that she was the one who'd lost her damn mind. "That's not a thing."

"It is most definitely a thing." She leaned back on her hands and stared at the sky. The move arched her back and pressed her breasts against the fancy tank top she wore. It was made of some kind of drapey fabric that looked soft and shiny, and it highlighted the fact that he seriously doubted she was wearing a bra. "You're too young to just give up."

"It's not about giving up." Though he didn't expect Hope to understand that. He'd checked up on her a few times since the accident, and every single time he was amazed at the things she'd accomplished. Life had kicked her in the teeth and she'd come back swinging. She'd taken two years off and then attended the University of Texas and graduated with honors. She ran her own successful consulting business to work with companies that wanted to set up scholarships and nonprofits.

She shifted to look at him. "It looks like giving up from where I'm sitting." She continued before he could respond, not that he knew what the fuck he was supposed to say to that. "Are you happy?"

What the hell kind of question was that? "I'm getting by."

"That pretty much answers that." She gave him a bittersweet smile. "I should have come back before now to check on you—or at least knock some sense into you, since apparently you need some tough love."

Check on him like he was her responsibility, when the truth was he was the one to blame for everything bad that had happened to her. "You worry about your own life and leave me to worry about mine."

"Because you're doing such a stand-up job of living it?"

He glared. "What in the fuck is that supposed to mean? It's great that you're happy—better than great. You deserve that and more. How I go about my business isn't any of yours."

"You're right. I know you're right." She sighed, the sound so small that he wanted to wrap his arms around her. It was more than the sigh, though. They'd dated for two years back in high school, been each other's firsts across the board. Apparently even after all this time, his body still remembered the feel of hers and craved it like crazy. He just hadn't been aware of it until she was sitting here next to him.

That's a goddamn lie.

The truth was he'd never stopped craving her in his arms and in his bed. He'd just stopped deserving her around the time John took his last breath. A person didn't come back from something like that, and no matter how well Hope had done with her life, that didn't change the fact that he'd taken things from her that were downright unforgivable.

Needing to get them onto solid ground—though he doubted that was a possibility at all—he said, "What's brought you back to town?"

"Work. Sort of." She pulled at the hem of her skirt, lifting the fabric enough for him to catch a glint of scar tissue on her calf. She hadn't done it on purpose—that he was sure of—but the reminder still struck him cold to the core. Oblivious, Hope continued. "Mom and Dad have been talking about doing a scholarship for John for years. They got in contact with the mayor and the principal of the high school and the city council and basically whoever would listen, and they've got a fund set up. So I'm here to get the details ironed out and officially announce it."

It made sense that she'd come back here for John. If he'd had a chance to stop and think since she showed up, he would have come to that conclusion on his own. Daniel quietly smothered the little voice inside him insisting that she'd really come back here for *him*. She hadn't. End of story. Allowing himself the fantasy would only make the truth hurt more.

And the truth was that any possibility of a future between him and Hope Moore was as dead as her brother.

Chapter Three

Hope should have known Jules had an ulterior motive for inviting her to dinner. As soon as she'd seen the cars in front of the house, she'd realized something more was going on, and she'd refused to get out of the truck until the other woman spilled. So she'd been able to brace for the knowledge that she'd see Daniel—as much as anyone could brace for seeing the man she once considered the love of her life.

Judging from the tension lining his shoulders, he hadn't had the slightest clue that his cousin had been meddling. In fact, everything about Daniel seemed to be tense these days. There were new lines around his mouth—deep brackets that she doubted came from smiling—and it was obvious that he spent significant time in the sun from how dark his normally tanned skin was.

It didn't detract from his looks, though.

Instead, it was almost like he'd been honed down and purged in a fire, coming out a leaner, meaner version of himself. Considering what she'd picked up from Jules, that was probably more accurate than anything else she could have compared it to. His thick black hair was longer than it had been, almost shaggy, and his dark eyes were downright haunted.

Hope bit her lip, wondering what she was supposed to do to help. He obviously wasn't happy to see her, and a part of her couldn't help feeling a little disappointment.

That's not why she'd come back. *He* wasn't why she'd come back, though she'd be a liar if she said the thought of running into her old flame hadn't crossed her mind. But that's exactly what Daniel was to her—what he had to be. Ancient history.

They'd had a chance to live the American dream that they'd always imagined, but instead of walking away from that car crash stronger, they'd been broken completely. Even if she wanted to magically bounce back from that, it was too late.

Maybe if he'd returned her calls after he came to visit her in the hospital…

But the time for maybes was long gone.

She was here to finally do what she'd promised her parents and set up John's trust. As much as she'd wanted to avoid coming back into town, avoid driving down Interstate 10 again and seeing the spot where their car went off the road, it was time.

Not a moment too soon, if the intervention Jules had mentioned breezily was something the Rodriguez family was actually planning. She didn't know if Daniel was really that badly off or if his parents and aunts and uncles and cousins had gotten together and riled themselves up into making it *a thing*.

She had to do something, she just didn't know *what*. She couldn't leave town again without at least trying to help him work through things—and getting his family off his back. She promised herself that right then and there.

"Whatever you're thinking, knock that shit off right now, darling."

The sound of his old nickname for her settling in the air between them temporarily shocked her into saying something she never would have otherwise. "I do what I want."

He turned to face her fully, brows lowered. It should have looked ridiculous with that tiny puppy bounding around him, into his lap and back out again, but something inside her quivered as a result of being pinned down by that expression. She couldn't quite tell if that was a good thing or a bad thing, though. Daniel leaned in, so close she wasn't sure of the heat she felt was coming from his body or the summer night around them. "That line never worked on me."

"It never worked on *anyone*." For one eternal second they were back there, in the world before.

Then he shook his head like he was waking from a dream. "I'm glad you're setting this thing up for John. It's football based?"

"Yeah." Her brother had gotten a full ride to the University of Texas when he graduated high school, and he'd been in his junior year of college, back home for the holidays, when the wreck took his life. So much potential, snuffed out in the space of a minute. The familiar ache settled in her chest, but it wasn't as strong or present as it had been this afternoon.

When she'd woken up in that hospital bed and realized her brother hadn't survived, she'd vowed to herself that she'd do whatever it took to make sure the gap created by John's death was filled. It'd been an irrational promise, but she'd stuck with it. Every time physical therapy brought her to the brink of despair, she fought it off because John never would have given up. And then she'd finished college with honors because that's what John had been on his way to doing.

She had no interest in being a lawyer—and she wasn't particularly good at arguing her point when strong emotions were involved—so she'd gone into the private sector, helping people and companies with too much money on their hands set up foundations and scholarships to help people who could actually *use* that money. Most of them were doing it for the tax write-off, but their motivation didn't matter—what they were doing did.

But those foundations and scholarships weren't personal. This one was. This felt like the final accumulation of what she'd been working toward—giving other kids from Devil's Falls a chance to follow the same path John had been on—to succeed where his life was cut short. "Football based, and they have to have the same kind of grades he did. There are other factors, too, but ultimately it'll be up to the discretion of the town council."

He gave a short nod. "It's good that you're doing this."

Funny, but he didn't sound particularly happy about it. Then again, he hadn't sounded happy from the moment she'd walked through that door. She took a deep breath. It was time to talk about that forbidden subject, the one that lay like a pulsing wound between them. Maybe getting it all out in the open would help him. "Danny—"

He pushed to his feet. "As fun as this has been, I've got to go."

"*Go?* You just got here." She struggled to her feet as he scooped up Ollie and started around the back of the house. Hope cursed under her breath, muttering about insane men, and hurried after him. The ground was too uneven to actually catch up with him, but she rounded the corner almost on his heels. Which was right about the time that her ankle wobbled, twisting her weak knee and sending her sprawling.

She hit the ground with bruising force, but that was nothing compared to the embarrassment making her wish the dirt would just part and suck her under. *Stupid rookie mistake. You know better than to run around over uneven ground.* But then, her common sense had always had the nasty habit of taking a backseat when Daniel was around.

Strong hands grabbed her under her armpits and pulled her to her feet. "Christ, Hope, what the fuck do you think you're doing?" Daniel patted her down, brushing the dirt from her shoulders and sides and chest. He froze when his hands touched her breasts, and the heat of her blush from her embarrassment turned into something else entirely. She swallowed hard, taking a deep breath that pressed her against his palms more firmly. The fabric of her shirt was thin enough that she could feel the calluses on his palms, and her nipples budded from the contact, her body going soft and warm as if she was some twisted sort of Pavlov's dog and Daniel was her bell.

When he spoke again, his voice was deeper. "Are you hurt?"

Not in the way you mean. "I don't think so." Her knee throbbed like the dickens, but she wasn't about to admit that to him. And, to be fair, it hurt the majority of the time to one degree or another. But admitting that meant he might stop touching her. She leaned into him and licked her lips, her gaze dropping to his mouth. "Danny…"

"When you look at me like that, I forget all the reasons I promised to leave you alone."

Why the hell would he promise to leave her alone? That was the stupidest thing she'd ever heard. She clenched her teeth together to keep from telling him so and ruining the moment. There would be plenty of time to rip Daniel a new one…later. "Then don't." She grabbed the front of his T-shirt and pulled him against her, stretching up to kiss him. He resisted for a grand total of one second.

And then he took control.

Daniel brought his hand up to yank her ponytail holder out and tangle in her hair, simultaneously picking her up and backing them up against the house. And then he was there, his body pinning her in place, his thigh wedging between her legs, providing a delicious pressure against where she felt most empty. He took possession of her mouth, his tongue teasing her lips open and stroking against hers in a way that had to be designed to make the top of her head explode.

He used his grip on her hair to tilt her head back and kiss down her neck. "If I was a better man, I'd leave you alone."

She didn't have words to respond, not with him tracing her nipple through her shirt with his thumb. Hope moaned and pulled him closer, trying to think clearly enough to know what to say—or not to say—that would ensure this didn't stop. Then his free hand slid beneath her shirt and she forgot about talking at all.

"No goddamn bra." He cupped her breast, his calluses creating delicious friction against her nipple. "What the hell were you thinking, showing up here with no bra?"

This, at least, she knew how to deal with, even if she was out of practice. Hope lifted her chin and met his gaze, half sure she was imagining the possessive look she found there. "I'm not wearing panties, either."

"What. The. Fuck?" Immediately, he fisted the fabric of her skirt, lifting it high against her thighs and sliding his hand between her legs. "Christ, darling, you really know how to send a man to his knees." He cupped her, his fingers sliding through her wetness but not penetrating her. It felt so good, but not nearly good enough, all at the same time. "But then, you always did."

At their feet, Ollie yipped, breaking the spell. Daniel exhaled a harsh breath. "This is a mistake."

It was. She knew that, and she didn't care. This would never happen again, and knowing that made her feel totally and completely out of control. Here in this moment, nothing seemed real but them, and she wasn't ready for it to end. Not yet. She covered his hand with her own, holding him in place.

"Danny, please." She licked her lips. "Please don't stop."

. . .

Daniel couldn't deny her if he wanted to—and he sure as fuck didn't want to. He ignored the pup at his feet and pushed a finger into her, watching her face. She clenched around him, her inhaled breath the sweetest thing he'd ever heard. He pumped gently, feeling anything but, trying to remember to take it slow. She was hot and tight and already drenched, her breasts rising and falling with each exhale.

"Danny…" She cupped him through his jeans. "Now."

This was so damn wrong. It had never been like this with them. Hot beyond belief, yes. But not quick, not rushed, not harsh in any way. But harsh was the only thing Daniel knew anymore.

He kept pumping, spreading her with his fingers while he used his free hand to undo his jeans. His cock sprang free, and it took everything he had to pause. "Hold on, darling." He grabbed his wallet out of his back pocket, riffling through it for the condom he'd put there…at some point. He hesitated. "Damn, it's been—"

"I don't care. Put it on." She kissed him, reaching between them to stroke him once, twice, a third time, until he had to get the fucking condom on or he was going to come in her hand. If he was going to get one more shot at being inside Hope Moore, he wasn't going to ruin it.

He tore open the condom wrapper with his teeth, refusing to stop touching her, though he had to let go for a second to roll the damn thing on. It took too long, but he had both hands free when he was done, and she'd kept her skirt lifted for him. *Good girl.* He stepped into her, pressing her against the wall. It struck him again that this was twelve different kinds of wrong to be doing her against the wall of his best friend's house, but he was too far gone to care.

Hope kissed him, hopping up and putting her legs around his waist, and that was that. He adjusted his angle and pushed into her, his entire body shaking at the feeling of her pussy clamped so tightly around him. "Jesus, darling. I'd convinced myself I'd imagined how good you feel." He cupped her ass, lifting her up and slamming her down onto his cock.

I missed this. I missed you.

Even in the throes, he couldn't say it aloud. She wasn't staying, and he had no business throwing their past in her face. *Stop thinking and just enjoy this, damn it.* He kissed her, giving himself over to the feel of her thighs squeezing his hips, her nails digging into the back of his neck, the breathy little moans that she made in the back of her throat. All too soon, her body tightened around him, her pussy milking him as she came with a soft cry. Daniel tried to hold on, to prolong it, to keep going, but it was too good. He pinned her against the wall and pounded into her, urged on by the building pressure in his balls. He came with a curse that damn near buckled his knees and caught himself against the rough wood.

Long seconds ticked past, their breathing slowly returning to something resembling normal. He ran a hand over her ass and down her thigh, pausing when the skin changed just above her knee, becoming rough and almost twisted.

Hope jumped like he'd electrocuted her. "Oh, God." She shimmied until he set her on her feet, quickly stepping away from him and adjusting her clothing.

He hated that, though he didn't blame her. He couldn't get the feeling of that scarred skin out of his head, and the knowledge that he'd been the one responsible sat heavy in his chest. He took a step back and went to get rid of the condom.

Daniel knew something was wrong the second he touched his cock. He pulled the condom off—the *ripped* condom. "Oh, shit."

Chapter Four

What the hell did I just do?

Hope stared at the broken condom and suddenly the night was closing in on her and she couldn't catch a full breath. *Oh, no. Oh my God.* She tried to think past the rushing in her ears, but the panic cresting inside her made it all but impossible. "I'm on birth control." Sort of. The truth was that she'd just gotten a prescription last week and started them today—well, technically yesterday. *It shouldn't have happened like this.*

It shouldn't have happened at all.

There was no excuse for the stupidity of what she'd just done. She looked around wildly, half expecting a brilliant solution to materialize in front of her. There was nothing but the stars and the field around the house, both so painfully familiar and yet completely different. It was *all* different. All wrong.

She never should have followed Daniel through the backyard, but she'd been so blind, so sure she could fix everything like she always did. "I have to go."

"Hope…" Daniel sighed. "Yeah, you should. Let me give

you a ride."

That was the *last* thing she needed. Even with all evidence pointing to her having no common sense when it came to this man, it was like she was eighteen again, rushing headfirst into every situation, heedless of the danger. She'd just more than proven that she couldn't trust herself to keep control, which meant she needed to stay away from him in situations like this.

Situations like what*? We're at a party at his cousin's house and ten feet from half a dozen other people. It's not like I followed him home.*

Ollie chose that moment to start barking, and they both spun around as Adam walked around the side of the house. He stopped short when he caught sight of them, and even in the shadows, Hope could see the way his gaze jumped between them, his eyes widening for half a second before he got control of himself. "You two okay out here?"

"Fine."

Adam and Daniel stared at each other in a way she'd never seen before, almost calculating. Like there was a line they were on opposite sides of. Hope didn't like that. She didn't like that one bit. They were best friends—had been since they were kids. She refused to be something that came between them. She smoothed back her hair, belatedly realizing her hair tie had disappeared into the darkness. *Damn.* "We're good. I was just coming back inside to find Jules. I'm kind of tired and I want to head to the bed-and-breakfast."

"Hope—"

Adam stepped forward, angling so he stood between her and Daniel. "I'll give you a ride. I've got the keys to Jules's truck."

"Perfect." She honestly didn't care who was behind the wheel as long as she was putting some distance between herself and Daniel. She needed to *think*, and it was impossible to do that with her body still beating in time with the pleasure he'd brought her and his presence overwhelming her while he was just standing there.

She wasn't back for good. It wasn't fair to get tangled up with him. No matter how she could rationalize it, she'd never be able to have no-strings-attached sex with Daniel. She just wasn't capable of it.

So she ran.

Like a scared kid.

Hope took a few careful steps back. "I'll see you around, Danny." Then she hightailed it for Jules's truck. She didn't stop to think that it might be yet another stupid idea until Adam got behind the wheel and cranked the engine on.

He barely waited until they were off the dirt drive to start on her. "Why are you back in town, Hope?"

"What?" She jerked back, stung. "I'm here for the scholarship in John's memory."

"That's all well and good—if it were true. But you could set that shit up down in Dallas without ever setting foot back in Devil's Falls, and you damn well know it."

She crossed her arms over her chest. "I have half a dozen meetings set up tomorrow alone and—"

"Meetings you could hold over the phone." He didn't look at her, but the judgment in his voice hurt. A lot.

It was a fight not to hunch down in the seat. "If you didn't want to see me, you didn't have to offer to drive me."

"Fuck, that's not it." He scrubbed a hand over his face. "I'm happy to see you, kid. Really, I am. I've missed you like crazy—we all have—but this isn't about John. This is about Daniel." He didn't give her a chance to jump in, not that she knew what she was supposed to say. Things with Daniel were complicated, and not in a good way.

Adam turned onto the highway leading into Devil's Falls. "I don't judge you for not coming back. Fuck, I left, too, and I had every intention of staying gone. I'm sure it's hard being back here and seeing John everywhere."

She knew exactly what he meant. She might have been the kid sister, but she'd tagged along through most of their grade school adventures, and then again once she hit sixteen and Daniel finally woke up and realized she was totally in love with him. *Daniel.* Seeing him and Quinn and Adam together only brought into relief the missing piece, but there was comfort in knowing that those three were here in Devil's Falls, still friends despite everything. Still living and loving and maybe occasionally getting into trouble for old times' sake.

"Then what's the problem?"

"You goddamn well know what the problem is. You've moved on with your life, left the past where it belongs. Daniel hasn't." He finally looked at her, the lights of an oncoming car illuminating his face. "Despite not having seen you in a hell of a long time, I still love you like a sister, Hope. But that doesn't mean I'm going to stand by and watch you grind what's left of Daniel into the ground when you leave again."

"That's not fair." She couldn't dredge up any anger. Adam could be a dick, but that's not what this was. He was worried about Daniel. It seemed *everyone* was worried about Daniel. "I didn't come back here to mess with him."

"Maybe not, but you being back is going to do exactly that." He headed into town, pulling to a stop right next to her car in front of Cups and Kittens. "If you care about him even a little after all this time, stay the hell away from him, Hope. I mean it."

She stared at the dashboard, wondering when it had all gone wrong. *Oh, yeah, right around the time my skirt hit my waist.* "I came back to help."

"You won't help Daniel. You're only going to make it worse."

Her throat tried to close, but she managed to speak past it. "Some things don't change. You can be so damn mean sometimes, Adam."

"Yeah, I know." He sat back. "But it's the truth. You've been doing well. Don't look at me like that, of course I've followed up on you over the years—you're the little sister I never had by blood. Hell, Hope, you're doing better than well. I'm fucking proud of you."

Her eyes burned, and she blinked a few times, trying to tell herself that it was because of the heat and not because she was actually tearing up. She'd always considered him and Quinn brothers while they were growing up, though she'd thought those relationships had broken at the same time as hers and Daniel's. Adam had disappeared off to do the rodeo circuit, and the most she'd heard from Quinn was a snarky Christmas card every year. "I didn't know."

"I didn't exactly announce it. That's on me."

Those things went both ways. She'd followed his rodeo career, but she'd never seen him ride live. The thought of seeing one of the men she cared about getting thrown from the back of a furious bull...she couldn't handle it. "I promise I didn't come back here to cause problems."

"I know, kid. Trust me, I know. And if you were planning on staying, I wouldn't be warning you off him—you two were always good together."

Yeah, they had been. Right up until he stopped returning her calls and forced her to move on with her life without him. Hope took a shuddering breath. "Things change."

"Some things. Not this." He got out of the truck and walked around to open her door. She hopped down and squeaked when he pulled her into a hug. "I missed you, Hope. We all did."

She recovered quickly and hugged him back. "I missed you guys, too."

He let her go and ruffled her hair, the move one he'd repeated thousands of times before. "I'll follow you to the

B&B and carry your bags up."

"It's fine." She was already heading around the car for the tailgate. "I've got it."

"There's no shame in asking for help."

She went ramrod straight and turned to glare at him. She didn't want *anyone's* pity, let alone that of a man she respected and loved like a brother. "I am *not* helpless, and I'm more than capable of wrestling a stupid suitcase into my room. Leave it alone."

"If you say so." Adam held up his hands. "Kid, I don't know how they do things down in Dallas, but you're back in Devil's Falls—around here, we help each other out, and it's not seen as a criticism."

She knew that—just like she knew that she was being rude for snapping at him. She was just so damn used to people looking at her screwed-up knee and seeing someone less than whole. And, truth be told, her leg was hurting her something fierce right now, the pain radiating all the way to her hip. All she wanted to do was go up to her room and lie down for a little while and just process everything that had happened.

But that didn't mean she should be taking it out on Adam. "I'm sorry."

"Don't be." He gently nudged her aside and grabbed her suitcase. "It's weird being back in town, huh?"

"The weirdest."

Fifteen minutes later, she was all checked in and Adam was gone, leaving her in peace. At least in theory. In reality, she kept replaying the last few hours and wondering when her well-intentioned plan had jumped the rails. The goal had always been to come back here, get some closure, and go back to her life in Dallas, feeling better about everything. About putting that nagging what-if question to rest, once and for all.

Instead, here she was, having just had a quickie with her ex against the side of a house, getting ripped a new one by a man she considered a brother, and going to bed wondering what the hell she'd been thinking.

Coming back to Devil's Falls had been a horrible mistake.

• • •

Daniel spent the next few days half sure that Hope would randomly show up on his doorstep. By the time he realized she had no intention of doing that, almost a week had passed. *I don't even know how long she's in town for.* He should just let it go. It was no wonder she didn't want to see him. Their past aside, she'd barely been back in town an hour and he'd been fucking her against the wall like she was...well, anyone other than Hope Moore.

Dirty, filthy sex wasn't what they did.

Hell, they didn't do *any* kind of sex these days.

Except they had.

He shook his head and opened the driver's door so Ollie could jump into the truck. She didn't quite make it, and he was forced to leap forward to catch her before she flopped onto the ground. "Damn, girl." At least between the pup and work, he'd had more than enough going on to keep him from having too much time to wonder what Hope was doing. If she was revisiting their old haunts. If she was spending any amount of time down at the diner.

If she'd visited her brother's grave.

He should just leave it alone. If she wanted to see him, it was child's play to figure out where he was. He hadn't asked her to come back. Damn it, he'd been doing just fucking fine before she showed up. And yet there he was, starting his truck and heading away from his house. The entire time he sat there and told himself this was a mistake. He didn't have any right to make demands on Hope's time—not after what happened thirteen years ago, and not after what happened a week ago.

But he wanted to.

He drove into town and then ended up parking outside Cups and Kittens because cruising Main Street was for idiot teenagers and stalkers, neither of which he wanted to be. *Yep. Just visiting my meddling cousin. Right.* He pushed through the front door—and immediately regretted his decision to come here.

Ollie took one look at the pair of cats sunning themselves in the afternoon beam of light, yipped, and took off running. Daniel dived for her, but she evaded him like a pro, barking up a storm. The cats fled, jumping up onto one of those cat jungle things and out of reach, hissing and swiping, their hair standing on end while Ollie ran circles around the base.

"What's going on out here?" Jules came sprinting out of the back and skidded to a stop in front of the scene. "Oh, good lord."

Daniel scooped up the pup—who was still barking shrilly enough to burst his eardrums—and backed up. "Didn't stop to think this was a bad idea. Sorry."

"It's okay. Here, bring her into the back." She led the way back into the kitchen and shut the door behind them. Once he was sure there were no cats in the room, Daniel set Ollie down. She set to sniffing everything she came across, apparently having forgotten the drama she'd just started. Jules laughed softly. "Maybe we should have gotten you a cat."

"Nah, I'm more of a dog person." He hadn't planned on having a dog, but Ollie had grown on him in a big way. She was just so damn goofy. He crouched down and ran a hand over her back.

"So, what brings you into town?" Jules asked the question far too casually.

He thought about lying or making some lame-ass excuse, but they both knew why he was here. "You seen Hope around?"

"She left."

The bottom of his stomach dropped out, and he shot to his feet. "What?"

"Yeah." Jules shuffled her feet. "I guess she wrapped up stuff faster than she thought she was going to and headed back to Dallas yesterday."

I missed my chance. He knew he was half a second from weaving on his feet and brought his shit under control *fast.* He should have known that she wouldn't want to see him again before she left down. Why the fuck would she? She was missing her goddamn knee and her brother because of him, and the first thing he'd done after not seeing her for thirteen years was let things get out of control and use a condom that was far too old. They hadn't even had a chance to have the conversation where he explained that he was clean...

"I need her number." He didn't realize he was going to say it until the words were out of his mouth. He'd let things stand before, and he'd put enough distance between them that she'd eventually moved on with her life because that was what was best for her at the time. The thought of her being hurt and retreating because of what he'd done for a second time was too much to bear. He had to at least talk to her or let her yell at him. Something.

"I don't actually have it."

Of course she didn't. Why would she? He'd have realized that if he'd stopped long enough to think instead of just reacting. Daniel scrubbed a hand over his face. "It's probably for the best."

Jules bounced on her toes a little, practically wringing her hands. "I guess I should apologize. I didn't think things would go so sideways or I wouldn't have invited her to your surprise birthday party." She hesitated. "I know Adam got kind of pissy with you that night."

"It's fine." The thing was, he understood why Adam had

acted the way he had. Daniel would have done the same thing if he'd found one of his little cousins in the same position he and Hope had been in, and both Adam and Quinn viewed Hope as a little sister.

He scooped up Ollie and headed for the back door. "I'll see you around."

"Daniel."

He stopped and glanced over his shoulder at her. "Yeah?"

She was actually still, her expression painfully serious. "I really do miss you. We all do."

What could he say to that? He knew he was a miserable bastard, just like he knew that even being in the room with his friends was enough to bring them down. They tried to hide it, but it was the damn truth. For the longest time, he'd tried to fake being happy, but it hadn't worked. Nothing worked.

So he'd done them all a favor and started withdrawing more and more. Being alone kind of sucked sometimes, but he was getting used to it. Since he didn't see either himself or the circumstances changing anytime soon, he gave Jules a small smile and lied through his teeth. "I'll try to come around more often."

"No, you won't." She shook her head and waved him away. "Just don't get pissed when I'm showing up on your doorstep and intruding in your life."

"I wouldn't expect anything else." He walked through the door and out into the August heat. He tilted his head back, letting the sun beat down on him, wishing it could burn away the sick feeling in his gut. Hope was gone. Again. He didn't believe in second chances—not really—but if he'd been allotted one, it had slipped past him while he'd been stewing. He'd never see her again.

It's for the best. She can do better than a man like me, and we both know it.

The truth didn't make him feel a damn bit better, though.

Chapter Five

Hope pounded on the door for the third time, not caring that it was almost midnight or that all the lights were off or that no one knew she was back in Devil's Falls. After her initial panic attack earlier today, she'd been eerily calm while she finished her work, cleared her schedule for the weekend, got in her car, and started driving west. But now that panic was back—with interest. *Six weeks. It's been six freaking weeks. Too long.* Six weeks since her snafu with Daniel and the broken condom.

Six weeks and no period to show for it.

The dog started barking, and she pounded on the door harder, thankful that he lived out in the middle of nowhere, because she knew she was making a scene and she couldn't stop. "Open the damn door, Daniel!" She shouldn't have come back. She was an adult. She should have just put on her big-girl panties and taken every single pregnancy test in the three boxes she'd purchased earlier that day.

But the thought of facing the results alone in her Dallas apartment had nearly been enough to send her curling into a ball she might never crawl out of. It wasn't right. She was the strong one, the woman who didn't meet an obstacle that she wouldn't find her way over, under, or around. She'd stopped leaning on anyone when she was eighteen and realized that the temptation to let the people around her carry the heavy weight was just another crutch that she refused to give in to.

All that didn't change the fact that she couldn't face this without him.

What if it's positive? Hope paused in her knocking and shuddered. That wasn't news that should be delivered over a phone call. Not to mention she didn't even *have* his number anymore. It wasn't like he'd been all that eager to give it to her after the way things had gone last time she was in town.

The door flew open to reveal Daniel, and she couldn't even stop to appreciate the sight of him wearing a pair of low-slung sweats or the fact that he'd seriously filled out since he was twenty-one. Appreciating her ex's hot body was what got her into this mess to begin with. Hope shouldered her way past him into the house, her heart beating too fast, her breath harsh in her throat.

"Hope?" He blinked and closed the door behind her. "What are you doing here? What's wrong?"

She laughed, high and hysterical. "I'm in trouble. I think. Or, rather, *we're* in trouble." That truth had been solidifying all day in the back of her mind. She wasn't late. Ever. There was only one reason she would be now.

Oh, God.

He stepped in front of her and put his hands on her shoulders. "You're not making any sense. Slow down."

There was no slowing down. Not until she knew for sure. Hope ducked out of his hold, knowing she was acting crazy and unable to stop. She grabbed her purse and went to her knees to dig through it, coming up with all three boxes. She looked up in time to see Daniel register what they were, and the shock on his face would have been comical under any other circumstances.

She went still, her chest trying to close in on itself. "I didn't take them yet."

"I see that." He came over to crouch in front of her. Daniel searched her face. "You could have called. I still have the same number. I would have come to you."

It hadn't even occurred to her that he'd had the same number. The last time she'd needed him, he hadn't been there for her. As much as she was at peace about her past—mostly—that rejection was always lurking there. He'd broken her trust, and she couldn't guarantee that he wouldn't do the same thing again. "I'm scared, Daniel."

He finally reached out and touched her knee. Her good knee. "What can I do?"

How about invent a time machine and go back to make sure this never happened? She didn't snap at him. He was asking an honest question, so she owed him an honest answer. "There's nothing you *can* do. It's already done."

He took one of the boxes out of her hand and opened it. She had the irrational urge to snatch it out of his hands, because opening it felt like the point of no return. Daniel unfolded the instructions and scanned them. "It says here that for best results, you need to take it first thing in the morning."

"That is how pregnancy tests usually work."

He shot her a look. "I wouldn't know." Before she could say something else to make the situation worse, he pushed to his feet and offered his hand. "Come on. You've got to be exhausted."

She didn't want his pity, and she wasn't sure she wanted his help at all. But since she'd come all this way, it was the lowest idiocy to throw a bitch fit now. So she took his hand and allowed him to pull her to her feet. He started down the hallway toward three closed doors. "Come to bed. You need to sleep."

Everything hurt. Her head, her chest, most especially her knee. She'd spent more hours today pacing than she cared to count, and it had taken its toll. But if she said anything, Daniel would freak out, and she didn't have it in her to dance around his guilt tonight. "Do you have a spare bedroom?" She wasn't willing to strip herself naked for him, emotionally or otherwise. She was too raw, too overwhelmed.

His step hitched, but he changed directions, opening the door immediately to their right. "It's not much, but there's a futon in there."

His bed would be more comfortable, but the thought of being in Daniel's bed again was... Yeah, no. She'd deal with the futon. She walked into the room. "Good night." And then she shut the door in his face. Hope slumped onto the futon, every worry and pain screaming for her attention. She dropped her head into her hands, fighting back a complete and total breakdown.

She'd worked so incredibly hard to move on with her life—she'd even thought she'd succeeded. But the second she crossed the county line, she was right back in the midst of the past she'd tried so hard to leave behind.

. . .

Daniel didn't sleep. He didn't even try to. Instead he took Ollie into the backyard and let her run. In the past month, she'd proven herself more than capable of keeping up with him, her awkward puppy form starting to hint at the dog she'd become. It wouldn't be long before he could take her when he went out riding—after he figured out how to tone down her enthusiasm. He'd introduced her to Rita last week, and that encounter had been as memorable as it was problematic.

None of that mattered.

He scrubbed a hand over his face. Hope goddamn Moore

was in his guest bedroom. He could barely wrap his mind around it. And if she was pregnant... His body went hot and cold, fight-or-flight responses kicking in. *What the fuck am I going to do with a baby?*

You always wanted a few of them.

Before. Not now.

The universe had the most fucked-up sense of humor. He'd learned that the hard way time and time again, and it always managed to surprise him. All he'd ever wanted when he was in his early twenties was to marry Hope, settle down in a little farmhouse, and raise a family. That dream was long gone, and yet here she was, possibly pregnant with his child and back in Devil's Falls.

Her life is in Dallas.

If she was pregnant, she'd take his baby back there, half a state away from him.

No goddamn way. Daniel pushed to his feet and turned to face the house. It didn't matter how much time had passed—he knew Hope and he knew how her mind worked. She'd have a plan, even if she couldn't admit to herself that she had a plan. A plan that wouldn't include him, not this time. Well, fuck that. He had as much a right to decide that baby's future as she did.

He strode back into the house, fear and anger and something else entirely all tangled up inside him. He threw open the door to the guest bedroom. "If this is my baby—"

"Oh my God!" Hope screeched.

Daniel froze. Hope was sitting on the futon in her T-shirt and only a pair of underwear, her legs stretched out in front of her. The right was just as perfect as it had always been, but that wasn't what drew his gaze. He focused on her scarred leg, on the pocked flesh and scars running from several inches down her thigh all the way to her shin. "Hope—"

"Get out!" She grabbed the blanket off the back of the

futon and tossed it over the lower half of her body. "I know this is your house and all, but you don't get to just walk in here." Her voice was shrill and her movements jerky. If he hadn't known how messed up over this she was, that would have more than shown him.

And I let her just close herself away so she could stew.
Idiot.

He forced himself to take a mental step back and breathe. Yelling at her wasn't going to do anything but piss them both off, and a screaming match wasn't going to do either of them any good. "The baby."

"The theoretical baby."

"Darling, you wouldn't be here if you didn't think pretty conclusively that there was a baby." Every time he said those words, his gut lurched, and for the life of him he couldn't say if it was a good thing or a bad thing. "You can't take it away from me."

"If it's a baby, it's not an it." She clutched the blanket to her chest, glaring at him like he'd just personally insulted her.

He chose not to comment on the fact she was flip-flopping wildly right now about what she wanted. Daniel figured she was entitled. Actually, the more freaked out she acted, the calmer he felt. He could do this. It might not be planned, but he wasn't going to spit on the chance to make amends that fate had given him.

He just needed to bring Hope around to the idea of it. Tentative plan solidifying in his mind, he crossed his arms over his chest. "What do you need from me?"

"How about some goddamn privacy?"

"If I leave, you're just going to sit there and your mind is going to run in circles all night." The same thing he'd be doing. He motioned. "Come on. I think I have some tea stashed around here." As soon as he said it, he realized she couldn't just up and follow him. Guilt rose up and punched him in the gut. The baby thing had him so turned around, he'd actually forgotten that her leg had irreparable damage because of him. *Goddamn it.* It was almost enough to make him retreat, but he powered on. "If your knee is bothering you, I can carry you."

"No." The word came out sharp enough to cut. Hope shook her head. "You will not be carrying me anywhere, so get that idea out of your head right now. I'm more than capable of moving around on my own."

He waited, but she didn't move. "Did you want me to turn my back or some shit?" What if she fell over? He went cold. What if in falling she hurt the baby? Daniel took a step forward. "It's no trouble to carry you, darling. I've done it enough times."

"Touch me and lose your hand." She still didn't move from her place beneath the blanket, though her dark eyes were fierce. "I'm not an invalid, Daniel. I'm not some broken toy that you can cart around until it feels loved again. I've been like this almost longer than I was the other way. This is my reality, and I don't need your help, and I sure as hell don't need your pity."

Her reality.

Again, guilt tried to choke him. He fought it down, but only barely. He couldn't afford to let her drive him away, not when there might be a baby. "Would you like some tea or not?"

Hope shook her head. "I don't think that's a good idea right now."

Because he'd gone and fucked this up.

It struck him that he'd spent so much time fighting to distance himself from the people around him that he didn't know *how* to interact with people anymore. He'd pissed Hope off when he'd only been trying to help, because he was so damn clumsy with his attempts to comfort her. It used to be second nature to reach out and pull her close. Then again, she'd been in love with him back then.

A lot had changed.

Daniel backed out of the room and closed the door behind him, deciding that he needed to figure out what the fuck his plan was, because blundering through this was just going to ensure that Hope would drive back to Dallas at the first available opportunity and take his baby with her.

And this time she might not be back.

Chapter Six

Hope slept horribly, unable to get the look on Daniel's face out of her head. The one that showed up when he caught sight of her leg. It was all guilt and pity and something almost like disgust. She shuddered and rolled over to bury her face in the pillow. She hadn't been celibate for the last thirteen years, but she'd been very selective over who she'd let get close enough to actually see her 100 percent naked. She might be mostly at peace with her body, but she didn't need the kick in the teeth that came when a potential lover made their excuses to leave as soon as her pants came off.

It hadn't happened yet, but the fear never quite went away.

A five a.m. she sat up, her full bladder making it impossible to procrastinate any longer. Her leg still hurt like nobody's business, but she'd be damned before she limped her way to the bathroom. She'd powered through worse pain before, and no doubt she'd do it again, but she wasn't going to give Daniel an excuse to offer to carry her again.

It's not forever. I might have panicked in a big way and

come back here, but that doesn't mean I'm staying. Once this is over...

That was the problem. If she was pregnant, this wasn't something she could just smile and keep on keeping. They were talking about a *baby*. With Daniel. Hope pushed to her feet. She'd thought it was intense enough having her past tied to him in more ways than she cared to count. To have her future tied to him as well was just... She didn't know what it was, but it didn't make her comfortable in the least.

She opened the door—and screamed. "Oh my God, what's *wrong* with you?"

Daniel held up one of the pregnancy test boxes. "I know you, and now that you've had some time to calm down, you'd have no problem sneaking into the bathroom and taking this test without letting me know." He held the box just out of reach, still blocking the doorway. "If this is positive, that changes things, Hope."

She wasn't an idiot. It would change everything. Her mind couldn't quite encompass the possibilities, couldn't take a single step past taking the test. "Give me the test."

"I've made my point." He handed it over.

"Bully for you." Having this box in her hand meant there was no more opportunity for stalling. It was happening. She was going to walk into the bathroom, and when she walked back out again, there would be no more room for maybe. She turned to look at the single window in the guest bedroom. The sun hadn't even begun to creep past the horizon. If she was back in Dallas, she'd be on her way to morning yoga and thinking about the odds and ends she wanted to accomplish this weekend.

"Running won't help anything."

She turned back and glared, hating that he was standing there, appearing to be calm and collected while she was falling apart. "Get out of my way before I piddle on your floor like your damn puppy."

"Don't bite my head off." He moved out of the way, waiting until she was to the bathroom door before he responded, "And Ollie's house-trained, so you following her example wouldn't be so bad."

She resisted chucking the box at his face, but only barely. Instead, she very carefully shut the door and made a point of engaging the lock. The very last thing she needed was Daniel barging in to watch her pee on a stick, and if the stubborn look on his face was any indication, he was actually considering it.

Hope double-checked the instructions—as if they would have changed from the half a dozen times she'd read them in the grocery aisle—and took a deep breath.

It was now or never.

It took entirely too little time to finish and set the stick aside. She washed her hands, brushed her teeth using his toothpaste and her finger, and then went ahead and used his mouthwash for good measure. She was stalling and knowing she was stalling. Banging on the door made her jump half out of her skin. She swore under her breath and jerked the door open. "What?"

Daniel searched her face. "Well?"

She didn't have to turn around to know exactly where the test sat—on the back of the toilet. Taunting her. All she had to do was walk those three steps to it and see if that idiotproof thing read PREGNANT or NOT PREGNANT. Simple.

Except she couldn't take that first step.

Hope looked up at Daniel and had the sudden urge to just break down. If she did, he'd be there for her. He always had been.

Except that wasn't the truth. When she'd needed him the most, he *hadn't* been there for her. Leaning on him now was just setting herself up for disappointment and heartache. She'd had enough of both to last her a lifetime.

Hope took a careful step back, and then another. Using every ounce of willpower she had, she turned and picked up the test. Her breath left her lungs in an audible whoosh. "Shit."

Pregnant.

Maybe that whole idea of building a time machine to go back to before she thought it was a brilliant idea to have sex with Daniel was a legitimate idea after all.

A big, tanned hand appeared in her line of vision and took the stick from her. "Well, hell."

She looked up, the shock on Daniel's face startling a laugh out of her. It was that or start sobbing and never stop. She'd always been a damn fool when it came to this man, but this was so above and beyond as to be laughable. She clutched her stomach, her giggle turning into a string of them, each one more hysterical than the one before. "Oh my God. I can't. This is… Oh my God."

"Darling? Damn, girl, breathe."

She slumped against the wall. "This is so dumb. This kind of thing is supposed to happen to teenagers, not to adults who should know better. We're fifteen years too late." At least if they'd done it when they were teenagers, they would have had love on their side.

Love. And where did that get us?

She scrubbed her hands over her face, trying to get a hold of her emotional free fall. The wondering about what would have happened was pointless. It had happened. End of story. Now it was time to figure out a plan for moving forward.

A baby. What am I supposed to do with a baby?

Being a single mother had never been part of the vision she had for the future.

All at once, her determination to keep moving abandoned her, leaving her staring at the bathroom cabinet. It was like thousands of other bathroom cabinets out there, a light cedar color in a generic style. It was just so *wrong*—just like everything else about this situation. "How did this happen?"

"I'm sorry, darling. It's my fault." He crouched in front of her. "The condom…the sex…it was all me."

That was just like Daniel to try to take all the responsibility—and the guilt—onto his shoulders alone. "You know, that determination to play the martyr and absolve me from guilt is really annoying." She leaned her head against the wall. "Pretty sure I was there. Equally sure that I'd just switched birth controls and neither that nor the fact that you pulled a condom out of your *wallet* was enough to make me stop and use my common sense."

"All the same—"

"No, Daniel. Not all the same. It took the two of us to get into this mess. I'm an adult, same as you, and I knew what the possible consequences were." She just hadn't cared, because being kissed by Daniel after all those years had been too good to stop. It had seemed like it was worth the risk at the time.

Now?

Now, she just didn't know.

He offered her a hand. "We need to talk about this. Really talk."

That's what she was afraid of. She allowed him to pull her to her feet and shoved her hair out of her eyes. "We don't need to talk. I already know how this conversation goes."

"Do you now?"

"Yes." She charged on, talking so fast her words spilled over each other. "I'm keeping the baby."

He jerked back. "No shit. If anything else came out of your mouth, you were about to have a fight on your hands."

She kept going, ignoring him. "You're going to act all crazy and—"

"Here's some crazy for you, darling." He closed the distance between them, backing her against the wall. "That baby you're carrying is mine." He dropped his hand to her stomach, sliding beneath her shirt and splaying his fingers across her skin. "*Mine*. You made your choice when you came up here to take that test instead of doing it on your own in Dallas. You included me in this, so don't go crying about how unfair it is that I have a fucking opinion. You're having our baby, and you're staying here in Devil's Falls to do it."

What the hell? "Staying—"

He kissed her, stealing her words and taking possession of her mouth as if every part of her really was his. *It's not.* The token protest withered against the onslaught of sensation, the way his tongue stroked hers, igniting a need in her that she would have thought impossible considering the circumstances. He stroked her stomach, his thumb dipping beneath the waistband of her yoga pants to trail down her hip bone. She shivered, a moan slipping free.

Daniel twisted his wrist so he could slide his entire hand into her pants. He pushed a finger into her. The sensation made her moan again, and he ate the sound and then kissed around to her jaw. "You're so fucking wet for me. You always were." He pumped his finger in and out of her as much as he could. "Stay, darling. I'll have you coming more times than you can count. On my hand. On my mouth. On my cock."

Her entire body clenched at his words. It sounded so good, the temptation to let him make her feel good almost too much to resist. But if she let him win this one, she'd spend the next nine months—the next *eighteen years*—losing arguments. Not to mention her job—her *life*—was in Dallas. She'd been willing to make her plans around Daniel once before, and he'd dropped her like a bad habit the first time things went truly bad.

She couldn't go through that again.

It was hard to reach down and grab his wrist, harder than she could have imagined. "No."

Instantly, he pulled his hand out of her pants, though he

didn't back up. "The offer stands."

She'd just bet it did. Hope put her hands on his chest and gently pushed him back a step. "You can't sex me up to get your way. That's not how this works."

"Is that what you think I was doing?"

Damn, but he could play innocent entirely too well—that was, if she was inclined to forget what he'd just been whispering in her ear. She crossed her arms over her chest. "Yes, Daniel, that's exactly what you were doing. It's a dirty negotiation tactic if I ever saw one."

He grinned, the expression so unexpected, she was half amazed that her panties didn't hit the ground. "Can't blame me for trying." He raised his finger to his lips—the same finger that'd been inside her—and sucked it into his mouth, his gaze never leaving her face. He released it so suddenly, her knees actually went weak. "You'll change your mind."

"No, I won't." *I might.* Hope shook her head. *No, I won't.* Sex with Daniel was world ending, which was the damn point—she liked her world exactly the way it was. It would change now, and there wasn't anything she could do about that, but she could at least try to maintain control in the midst of all the insanity.

Which meant she couldn't let him have the upper hand. Not now. Not ever again.

She edged past him, well aware that he let her walk out of the room when all he had to do was kiss her again to crumble her admittedly pathetic protestation. She made her way down the hall and into the kitchen, stopping cold at what she saw there. Last night she'd been so distracted by acting like a crazy person that she hadn't really stopped to check out his place. Part of her had sort of just assumed that it was, she didn't know, *familiar.*

It wasn't.

She looked around the kitchen that could have been

in any cookie-cutter house around the country. There was nothing *wrong* with it, at least until she realized it was in Daniel's house. She moved around the breakfast bar, eyeing the empty counters, and opened a cupboard. There were two mason jar glasses in it, a stack of paper plates, and nothing else. She turned when he entered the room. "Is this a joke?"

"Is what a joke?"

"This." She motioned at everything. "This isn't your kitchen. It can't be." It was just too soulless.

"It's mine." He opened the fridge and winced, a reaction she shared when she saw how empty it was.

"But...how do you cook here with none of your old stuff?" Even right out of high school, he'd spent a good portion of his checks on fancy knives and food they'd had to drive into Pecos to get because the market in Devil's Falls didn't carry specialty items. Her favorite nights had been when they'd holed up in the little house he'd shared with his friends and he'd cooked for all of them. With his current setup, she doubted he could put together a peanut butter and jelly sandwich, let alone anything like the complicated dishes he'd loved.

He shut the fridge door. "I don't cook anymore."

That shocked her almost more than anything else that had happened since she woke up. Daniel didn't cook? It struck her that as well as she used to know the boy she'd dated, she didn't know a damn thing about the man standing in front of her.

And she was going to have his baby.

Chapter Seven

Daniel didn't like the way Hope was looking at him—as if he was broken. As if she saw through all the walls he'd built up around himself since that night thirteen years ago, and she knew that he wasn't anywhere near as okay as he liked everyone to think.

It set his teeth on edge. He didn't want pity from anyone— least of all from *her*.

To get away from the knowledge in her dark eyes, he'd do damn near anything. So he turned the tables. "We need to talk about the next nine months." And the next eighteen years. But he knew her well enough—or at least he used to— to know that coming at her with the rest of their lives on the table was a surefire way to get her to dig in her heels and shoot him down flat. He had no intention of rolling over and playing dead for her, but he'd let her think he was willing to settle for her sticking around for pregnancy and ease her into the idea of staying here for the long term.

Yeah, she had her job, and a life in Dallas that didn't include him or Devil's Falls, but he didn't much like the idea of her raising their kid hours away. The best he could hope for in that situation was every other weekend. Fuck that. Hope would stay here. He just had to figure out how the hell he was going to convince her of that.

He was reaching, and he damn well knew it. Daniel grabbed the carton of milk out of the fridge and mentally cursed. It had expired over a month ago. If she'd been freaking out in Dallas as much as she was last night and this morning, she hadn't been eating or taking care of herself. In order to convince her to stay, he had to prove he still knew how to do that.

So far, he was batting a thousand.

He dumped the milk into the sink and rinsed the carton out. As long as he wasn't looking directly at her, he could keep his cool. In theory. "How do you see this working?"

There, that was as nonthreatening as it could get.

Hope crossed her arms over her chest and raised her chin like she was stepping into the ring. "I know what you're thinking, and the answer is no. Devil's Falls is my past, and I'm keeping it that way. I have a life in Dallas, Daniel. A good one. This wasn't part of the plan, but that doesn't mean I'm going to drop everything to run back here and play little wife to you so that you can feel like you're fulfilling your duties. I'm not a duty, and neither is this baby. We both deserve better than that."

He couldn't argue that logic, but the truth was that it *was* his duty to do right by both of them. Daniel considered her. There had to be something he could say to get her to stop arguing long enough to see that this was the only way. "Where are your parents living these days?"

"San Antonio." She narrowed her eyes. "Why?"

That's it. That's the pressure point to push.

He had her, she just didn't know it yet. "It sounds like you have shit for a support system in Dallas."

"I have friends." From the defensive tone, she knew exactly where he was going with this.

"None of them that were good enough friends to be there for you when you took that test." Not that he was complaining on that note. She very well could have taken the test and moved on with her life in Dallas, and he never would have known the difference. The thought left him cold. He braced his hands on the breakfast bar and leaned forward. "Instead, you drove seven hours across the fucking state to my house to take it. Because you had no one else."

Hope sucked in a breath. "That's not fair. Unlike you, I wasn't going to hide from something that scared me. Yes, I came back here—back to *you*—to take the test, but it's only for the weekend. I'm going home tomorrow."

He ignored that, ignored the clock that instantly sprang into being, counting down until she walked out of his life again. If he thought too hard about it, he'd drive himself batshit crazy. "My point is that Devil's Falls has a built-in support system. Your parents are within easy drivable distance. I'm five minutes from *my* parents' place, and don't even get me started on my cousins." Every single one of them would lose their minds when they found out Hope was pregnant. She'd be so damn taken care of, she wouldn't have to lift a finger.

A part of him didn't want to tell anyone, solely so *he* could be the one seeing to her every need.

Rein it in.

Easier said than done. There was nothing but stubbornness on Hope's face, so he pressed his point. "What happens if you fall? Or there are complications with the baby? Are you going to call a fucking cab to come get you and then sit in Dallas traffic on the way to the hospital? If you're here, Doc Jenkins has no problem making house calls, and he's the same fucking doctor who delivered *you*, so don't tell me that some fancy city doctor is going to be better. They won't. They don't know you. Devil's Falls does."

He did.

He waited while she worked it out, her dark eyes unreadable. Finally, Hope turned away. "I understand what you're saying, but you're wrong. Even if you weren't—which you *are*—you're still doing this for the wrong reasons, Daniel. You know it, and I know it."

Wanting to fix things *wasn't* the wrong reason. She might not agree with him, but that was just the way it was. All he knew was that she had to be *here*, to be where he could keep an eye on her and keep her safe as she got farther along in her pregnancy. "Stay." He didn't care if he had to move heaven and hell and everything in between, he wasn't about to let her out of his sight any more than necessary. His theoretical comments weren't all that theoretical. She might be trying to cover it up, but he could see that she favored her injured leg, and that meant her chances of falling were higher than average, especially once she started getting big.

Daniel went still, the image of Hope with a large stomach filling his head. Seeing her big with *his* baby.

Fuck, I like that picture.

Right now, the most important thing was getting her to agree to stay in town at all. From there, he'd work on getting her into his home. He looked around. He didn't even know if he could call this house a home. It had never bothered him before—it was a place that kept the heat out in the summer and the cold out in the winter and the critters out while he slept. It had never felt lacking until now, with the woman he'd always thought he'd end up with standing there, looking as out of place as an angel in a dive bar.

It might not be the house he'd always promised that he'd build her, but he could spiff this place up into something better than it currently was.

He just needed her to agree to stay. "Give us a chance to

iron this out—a couple days. Stay through the week, and then we'll talk."

Her mouth dropped open. "What are you going to do, lock me up in the basement until I agree with you?"

That didn't sound like too terrible a plan, but he had a better idea. Daniel stalked toward her, knowing he was out of control and not caring. "I might do that. Or I might go over the list of perks again." He braced his hands on the counter on either side of her.

Her gaze rested on his mouth. "Your perks sound a whole lot like strings attached."

"Aw, darling, they might be exactly that." He leaned in, not quite touching her, but close enough that he could feel the warmth of her body and the way her breath shook. "But I can guarantee that you won't be worried about anything but the way my cock feels inside you."

She narrowed her eyes. "When did you get so damn pushy?"

He knew she was constantly doing a before and after comparison of him. Hell, he didn't even blame her. He was doing the same damn thing. When he was twenty-one, he'd been happy and carefree and so full of life it actually hurt to look back on that time. Now? Now he was half the man he used to be, and he wasn't about to start changing. He didn't deserve happiness, and he sure as fuck didn't deserve Hope, but if the universe was stupid enough to give him another shot with her, he wasn't a good enough man to walk away.

Deserving her or not, Hope was his. She just had to come to terms with it.

He tucked a strand of hair behind her ear, letting his fingers linger there. Everything else had changed, but he still knew exactly how to touch her to elicit a response. "When I find something worth fighting for."

"That's your problem." She turned and looked him

directly in the eye. "I was always worth fighting for."

He went still, the truth of her statement like a kick to the chest. "It wasn't right back then."

"Or maybe you were just too focused on sinking yourself into misery as fast as you could to realize the good you still had in your life." She saw too much. She always had. Back when she'd been a teenager, she'd been kind enough to back off before she revealed the fault line inside a person and forced them to face it. Apparently she wasn't too kind anymore. Hope pressed her lips into an unforgiving line—as unforgiving as the look in her eye. "John died in that car crash—*not me*. Except you didn't seem to understand that, because you were mourning my freaking leg as if that was all I was worth to you. A whole body." She pushed against his chest, not hard enough to move him, but hard enough to prove her point. "I hated you for a really long time."

"I deserved your hate." It was the simple truth. He'd taken everything from her. He'd hated himself for that, so it only made sense that she'd feel the same way.

Hope shook her head. "You're as much an idiot now as you were then."

And then she kissed him.

It caught him a little off guard—he hadn't expected her to be the one to make the first move, especially after the way the scene in the bathroom had gone down—but Daniel wasted no time taking control. He kissed down her neck, sliding his hands beneath her shirt and skating them up her body to cup her breasts. They filled his palms, familiar and yet not, all at the same time. He cursed. "Darling, the things you do to me." He nipped her collarbone. "I'm going to taste you, so if you're going to change your mind, now's the time to do it."

Her only response was to shove her yoga pants down to her knees.

He lifted her onto the counter and disentangled her right

leg from the pants so he could spread her fully. He stroked her thighs, pausing when his fingers met the scar. It brought up so many conflicting feelings in him. It was *his fault* that she had the damn thing, but that didn't mean he thought of her as less, the way she seemed to think. She was as beautiful now as she'd been at eighteen, and more confident despite her injury. Or maybe because of it. He had no idea.

All he knew was that at some point he was going to have to get up close and personal with her healed injury, and he was going to have to tread very, very carefully to avoid burning what was left of the bridge between him and Hope.

"If you apologize, I might actually kick you."

That snapped him out of it. As much as he wanted Hope, he had an ulterior motive for pushing her now. All getting distracted by her leg was going to do was fuck up his chance of convincing her to stay, in his house and in his bed. He jerked her to the edge of the counter, spreading her thighs wider. "Don't scream. You'll upset Ollie."

And then he did what he'd been fantasizing about ever since he walked out of her life. Daniel dipped his head and gave her center one long lick. She tasted better than he remembered, her body already shaking for him, so he used his thumbs to part her folds and licked her again, reacquainting himself with every inch of her.

"Oh."

He looked up her body to find her head thrown back and her chest rising and falling with each harsh breath. "Take off your shirt."

Hope wasted no time obeying, dragging the material over her head and tossing it away. And then there was nothing hiding her body from his gaze. He licked her again, savoring the way she shook. A tattoo curling around the bottom of her ribs caught his eye, but he was too distracted to read it.

He was tired of teasing her. He wanted to feel her orgasm

again, to know she was coming apart at the seams because of him. Daniel sucked her clit into his mouth, stroking the sensitive little nub with the flat of his tongue the way she'd always loved. Sure enough, before he had a chance to truly savor her, Hope cried out his name and shuddered, her thighs squeezing his head as she came. He gentled his touches, licks turning to kisses, turning to the slightest brushing of his lips against her. Only when she stopped shaking did he raise his head. "Stay, at least until we figure out what we're doing."

"You are...I don't even have words to describe what you are." She blinked and ran a hand over her face. "Is this how every argument is going to go?"

Hell, yes—at least if he had his way. Daniel dragged his cheek against her thigh. "You kissed me first."

"I was just trying to shut you up."

He laughed against her skin, not quite willing to let her go yet. "Well, that's one way to go about it."

Her smile died as she pushed him gently back and slid off the counter. "This doesn't solve anything. You know that, right? You can't just sex me into submission." She wrestled her pants back on, and he mourned the loss. Things were so much simpler when they were talking with their bodies instead of their words. No matter which way he lined things up, they were different people than they'd been when they dated. So much had changed since then, the terrain changed until he barely recognized the world around him.

But he knew her body.

He'd never stop knowing what made her hot and drove her crazy.

And he sure as fuck wasn't above using that to get what he wanted.

Chapter Eight

Hope climbed out of Daniel's truck and looked up and down the street. There were people around, but none of them seemed to be paying too much attention. That wouldn't last, but at least she had a slight reprieve to catch her breath.

In theory.

The truth was she didn't know what the hell was going on. One minute she'd been independent and asserting her need to create some distance between herself and Daniel, and the next his head had been between her legs. It was never like that with him before. It had been soft and sweet.

There was nothing soft and sweet about the man coming around the front of the truck to glare at her. He pointed. "I was coming to get your door."

"Either develop Superman abilities or come to terms with the fact that I can get my own damn door." She knew she was being rude, but she didn't care. She'd spent almost half her life taking care of herself without a man—without *him*—around, and she wasn't about to turn into a wilting flower just because he decided to walk back into her life.

Technically I walked back into his life.
And seduced him.
And messed up birth control.
And got pregnant.

It was kind of hard to maintain the moral high ground in this situation, but when it came to him sweeping in and taking over her life, it just wasn't going to happen. The sooner he figured that out, the better.

To end the conversation, she turned toward the storefront. The place looked exactly like it had when she was in high school. It was crazy. So much had changed—*she* had changed—and yet Devil's Falls was practically the same. It made it hard to differentiate between the past and present, too easy to fall back into the old rhythms she and Daniel had had. *I can't.* The minute she dropped her guard completely, he was going to have her quitting her job, moving in, and the man would probably go so far as to propose because he thought that it was the right thing to do.

Once upon a time, she'd wanted to marry Daniel Rodriguez. But not now. Not like this. Not when he was operating under some misguided belief that he was going to do right by her.

She moved away from him and into the store. The whole point of coming into town was to get some of the stuff she needed for the night—mainly food. She might be leaving in the morning, but she still had to eat in the meantime. She didn't know how he lived on the grand total of three items in his kitchen, but she wasn't about to start smearing mayonnaise on saltine crackers.

Hope froze, her stomach lurching. *Mental note—don't think about gross food combinations if you want to be able to eat breakfast.*

The woman at the counter looked up from the magazine she was idly paging through and gave a shriek fit to wake the dead. "Holy crap, Hope Moore, is that you?"

It took precious seconds to place the blonde, and by then she had hopped over the counter and was coming at Hope, arms spread for a hug. "Jessica Stroup?"

"The one and only." She engulfed Hope in a hug that popped her back. "It's been a million years! Why on earth are you back in this little shithole?"

She and Jessica had been on the cheerleading team back in high school, and the other woman had always had big dreams about heading west to L.A. and getting into modeling or acting. She was certainly beautiful enough for it. Hope smiled. "Visiting some old friends."

Jessica peered around her, her blue eyes going wide when Daniel pushed through the door. "Old friends *indeed*. We're going to have to go share a drink at the Joint and catch up. I know the bar isn't as fancy as the places you must be used to in Dallas, but it's what we have up here." She grinned. "You look a little frazzled, and I know I'm talking a mile a minute, so I'm just going to write down my number and you can give me a call. We don't have to drink. We can totally go for coffee or something. I'm off at three. Have you heard that Jules Rodriguez opened up a cat café down the street? Strangest concept I ever heard of, but it's loads of fun to go in there and play with the cats while you chat and drink coffee."

"Oh, ah, okay."

"I'm doing it again." She backed toward the counter, still smiling. "Go on and do your shopping. We can talk later."

Hope had forgotten how overwhelming Jessica was— but in a good way. It was actually kind of nice to have an interaction in town that wasn't fraught with undertones. She wasn't ready to confide about the pregnancy, but a break later today from Daniel's intense presence would be a good thing. Even though he didn't say anything, she felt him at her back as she grabbed a cart and headed down the first aisle.

Glowering.

It took all of ten feet before her patience ran out. "You have something to say, so say it."

He grabbed a can of soup off the shelf, seemingly at random. "I open doors, Hope. It's what any man worth his salt in the South does. It has nothing to do with what you can or can't do." Another can of soup hit the basket of the cart hard enough to bounce.

So they were back to that. She should have known. Daniel could be like a dog with a bone when something bothered him. She took a deep breath and turned to face him. If they were going to fight about every little thing, this would never work.

If she was going to be honest, her pride was as much to blame as his stubbornness.

Hope took a deep breath and tried to take the high road. "I get overly defensive. I'm sorry." She held up her hand. "I can't promise I won't snap at you again, but I'll try to relax about the door stuff."

He raised his eyebrows. "Just the door stuff?"

"Yes." It came out sharper than she intended, but damn, could he give it a rest for a few minutes? She knew he wanted her in his house permanently, just like she knew he might have appeared to drop it, but he was just planning a different method of approach. She was so damn tired, and it was only beginning. Hope turned to the row of cereal boxes in front of her. "Now, I'm starving, and arguing with you is burning more calories than I'm comfortable with. We'll talk when we get back to your place, and we'll come up with some sort of game plan." Staying in Devil's Falls for the next nine months was out of the question. She could do her job in a limited capacity online, but she really needed to be in the office. If she up and told them she was moving back to a little town no one had ever heard of, she might as well quit on the spot.

No. Absolutely not. She might have put her life on hold waiting for Daniel when she was eighteen, but she most definitely wasn't going to do it now because he was determined to pay penance by being with her.

She deserved better than that.

Both she and the baby did.

The look he gave her was downright indulgent. "Fair enough."

She hated how suspicious she was of him, but it was hard not to be in their current circumstances. Daniel never gave up a fight unless he chose to walk away, and he hadn't this time. That meant he was backing off only long enough to find a different approach to get her to do what he wanted.

They moved through the aisles without speaking, Hope pausing every few feet to consider what she felt like eating and Daniel throwing food into the cart seemingly at random.

She didn't know what to make of that, so she focused on what sounded good. It was so *strange*. She normally loved oatmeal in the morning, but when she picked up her favorite brand, she set it back without tossing it in the cart, that horrible nausea rising again. Instead, she ended up in the produce section, loading up on orange juice, fruit, and cucumbers. Through it all, Daniel shadowed her movements, a giant gray cloud warning of an impending storm.

Jessica managed to contain herself as they paid, but she slipped Hope her number with a smile. "It really would be nice to catch up."

As much as part of her wanted to keep her distance from everything Devil's Falls related, that goal wasn't realistic. She was leaving. She *had* to leave.

Hope forced a smile. "I'll call. I promise." And she would. Even though she and Jessica had lost contact after the accident, they'd been really close in high school. It would be nice to have a friend who knew the whole history, someone she could talk to who would understand why she was hesitating to cut Daniel out of her life, even now, after everything they'd been through. Her friends in Dallas were wonderful, but they would, to a person, tell her to get rid of him.

He loaded the groceries into the bed of his truck in short, jerky movements that belied the calm expression on his face. In an effort to keep the peace a little while longer, she waited for him to hold the door open for her instead of climbing into the truck like she was perfectly capable of doing. It wasn't until they were driving back out of town that he spoke. "My parents are going to want to know you're back."

"I'm not back."

"Yes, darling, you are. At least for today." He shot her a look. "You're just pissed that I pushed too hard about it and you don't want to give in, despite the fact that it's what you want. If you go back to Dallas right now, it's going to be a decision made out of spite."

She resisted the urge to cross her arms over her chest, but only barely. "I think I like you better when you're being irrational and pushy."

"It's a hell of a lot easier to say no to me when I am." He sounded too freaking cheerful for her blood pressure. How was he acting so calm when their entire lives had gone topsy-turvy? *Unless this is what he wanted all along...*

She shut that thought down *real* fast. This was an accident as a result of two consenting adults. She was as much to blame for the error in judgment as he was. Lord, she should be *happy* that he wasn't freaking out and blaming her and acting like this was the worst thing that had ever happened to him. "Daniel..."

He reached over and took her hand, the shock of his skin against hers stealing her breath. "We'll figure this out. I know it's not how you had your life planned out, but this is where we're at. It's not going to be easy, but what about life is?"

Too reasonable. Something is up.

She extracted her hand, because she couldn't quite think straight when he was touching her, and turned to look out the window. All the words coming out of his mouth were right, but there was something off about the delivery. It was like he knew the steps to go through but he didn't really believe that it would be that easy any more than she did. "I don't...I don't trust you anymore." It hurt to say that aloud, but it was necessary. Everything had changed, and that lack of trust was the most damning part. Hope took a deep breath. "I'm not staying. End of story. So whatever you're planning, knock it off."

"What makes you think I'm planning anything?"

Because he was too calm, too settled, when a few short hours ago he'd been totally and completely out of control. That switch didn't flip without a good reason, and she hadn't agreed to anything he wanted. Not really. She was leaving and that was that, and the fact he was so calm about it didn't sit well with her.

It all added up to trouble.

Even if she didn't know the specifics, she was smart enough to see which way the wind was blowing.

Chapter Nine

Daniel spent the next hour walking on eggshells. He knew he'd pushed Hope too hard that morning, and he was determined to figure out a better way to convince her that staying with him was the only option. Every single thing he said was the wrong thing, and he didn't know how to fix that. All he knew was that if Hope left in a couple days, she wouldn't be back.

So he gave them both a break and went outside to let Ollie run for a bit. The pup was in her element, running circles around him and then darting off to chase phantom animals, racing back and then starting the whole process over again. She, at least, didn't plan on leaving him the first chance she got.

Ollie barked again, wondering why he'd stopped playing, and he crouched down to ruffle her ears. He'd never considered himself underhanded before now, but he'd do worse than mess with Hope's car to get her to sit still long enough for him to find the right words to get her to stay.

Can't convince her from out here. He pushed to his feet and headed for the door, Ollie on his heels. Daniel opened the door—and then stopped when he heard humming deeper in the house. He sat down on the mudroom bench long enough to yank off his boots and then went in search of her. The living room was empty, but he found her in the kitchen, her phone set up to play some funky music he'd never heard before, her hips shaking as she moved around the stove, dumping ingredients into a casserole dish.

This could have been my life.

It still could be.

Without thinking, he crossed the distance between them and slid his arms around her waist. She went still as he rested his chin on the top of her head. "Damn, darling. I missed you."

"Danny—"

He turned her in his arms and framed her face with his hands. "We talk too much." And they never solved a damn thing doing it. Then he kissed her.

She went soft against him, her hands sliding down his chest to grab his hips and pull him closer. That was all the invitation he needed to tip her head back and deepen the kiss. Shit might be fucked up beyond all reason when it came to them, but at least they still matched up here.

Today she wore those damn yoga pants again. It didn't matter to him that he could see the ridges of her scar beneath the thin fabric, because they gave him a heavenly view of her ass whenever she turned around. And the stretchy fabric was more tease than barrier. He reached between them, rubbing the heel of his hand over her clit. "What do you say?"

She blinked at him, her brown eyes hazy with lust. "What?"

"This thing." He kept rubbing her, shifting so he could press a knuckle on either side of her clit, stroking up and down slowly. "I want inside you, darling. I want it so bad, it's been driving me fucking crazy." Her breath hitched, and he pressed his advantage. "You want it, too. You're so wet, I can feel it."

"I…" She bit her lip. "It's a mistake."

"Probably." *Definitely.* "But what's the worst that could happen?"

Her smile was bittersweet. "It's already happened."

Part of him hated that she thought getting pregnant was the worst thing that could happen, but now wasn't the time to start fighting about it. He'd have to show her that this was a second chance in disguise—a way to make things right once and for all—and the only way to get her to sit still long enough was an orgasm-induced coma.

It doesn't hurt that you've been in a permanent state of blue balls since you saw her last.

No, it didn't hurt one bit. Everything else might have changed, but he wanted Hope more than he wanted his next breath.

He slipped his hand into her pants, resuming the motion that had her quivering in his arms. "Might as well take advantage of me, then."

"Take advantage of *you*?" Her voice was a little breathy, but she managed to keep it together. Mostly.

"Mmm." He skimmed off her shirt, dropping it next to them and cupping her breasts. "Fuck. When I fill you with my cock, I want you naked. I want to see these beautiful breasts bouncing with every stroke."

"Arrogant."

"Realistic." He stroked her nipples with his thumbs, watching her face. "You know you're craving it. I bet you've been touching yourself remembering that night. Coming with my name on your lips just like you did then."

Her fingers dug into his biceps. "I hate you more than a little bit right now." She arched, pressing herself more firmly into his hands. "But I don't really care."

"Say yes."

"Yes." It was barely more than a whisper, but it might as well have been a yell with how the word reverberated through him.

Daniel spun her around, keeping a hold on her hip to make sure she didn't stumble, and shoved down her yoga pants. He reached between her legs from behind with one hand. "Christ, do you ever wear anything other than yoga pants?"

"Not when I'm lounging around the house, you jackass."

He delivered a stinging slap to her ass—more to get her attention than anything else. "When did you get so mouthy?"

"Right around the time you got so damn bossy." She braced her hands on the counter. "Now take me before I change my mind."

Daniel stroked a hand down her spine and palmed her ass. He undid his belt and jeans with his other hand. "How many times?"

"What?"

He pushed his jeans down and notched his cock at her entrance. "How many times have you fantasized about this?"

"Since we last had sex or since I was eighteen?"

The words hit him like a sucker punch to the gut. He sheathed himself to the hilt, using his hold on her hips to pull her back onto his cock. "Both."

She squirmed, breathing hard, but he wasn't about to let her move until he was damn well ready. Hope muttered a curse that made him smile despite everything. "A dozen times to the former, impossible to count to the latter."

He felt like crowing with a victory he sure as fuck didn't deserve. So he started moving, sliding out of her almost completely before slamming home again. "I've thought about you, too, darling. Over and over again, palming my cock and imagining it was your tight little pussy wrapped around it instead. It doesn't fucking compare. Nothing—*no one*—

compares to you." He reached around to rub on either side of her clit, his mouth against her ear, his chest pressed against her back. "You want to know why you couldn't stop thinking about me?"

"No." She shoved back against him, taking him deeper.

He licked the shell of her ear. "It's because this pussy is mine, darling. It always has been. It always will be."

"I…hate…you."

Daniel hitched her higher, running his free hand up to cup her left breast, pinching her nipple lightly. "Doesn't change a fucking thing. Now be a good girl and come for me."

He pressed three fingers hard against her clit and that was all it took. She cried out, her pussy spasming around him and her entire body shaking. He leaned back to grab her hips, pounding into her, chasing his own orgasm. Pressure built in the base of his spine, and though he tried to fight it off as long as he could, it was just too fucking good. He came so hard his knees buckled. "Holy shit."

And then there was nothing to do but lean against the counter, covering her, and relearn how to breathe.

Hope didn't give him much opportunity. She ducked out from beneath his arms and yanked her pants back into place. "You…I can't…God, *I hate you*."

He turned his head to watch her snatch up her shirt. "You're welcome for the orgasm."

"Don't start that crap with me. I agreed to sex. I did not agree to you doing the equivalent of peeing on my foot. I am not yours, Daniel. I haven't been for a long time and I never will be again."

• • •

Hope was so furious, she could barely think straight. *How dare he?* And she'd walked right into it, which was the most unforgivable part of the whole mess. She shoved out the front door, making it a whole three steps before Ollie rushed around the side of the house, barking happily. The dog ran circles around her, making it impossible to take a step without worrying about stepping on her.

Good lord. The dog was attempting to herd her back into the house.

She propped her hands on her hips and glared. "I know what you're doing, and I don't appreciate it any more than I appreciate what *he's* doing."

"Careful there—you're going to hurt her feelings, and I've never seen a canine that can mope quite as effectively as Ollie."

Deep down, she'd known that he'd follow her out here. She needed time to wind down, and Daniel wasn't going to give it to her. He'd just keep pushing and prodding and steamrolling until she either caved or exploded. Right now, the latter was looking pretty damn attractive.

She spun to face him. The fact that he looked rumpled and sexy only made her crazier. It would be so incredibly easy to stop fighting and let him steamroll her. He wasn't saying anything she didn't want to hear. But that was the problem—she no longer trusted Daniel Rodriguez. A baby. A catastrophic leg injury. Both were world-altering events, and he'd dropped her like a hot potato after the first one. Who was to say he wouldn't do the same thing after the other the second he stopped to think too hard about it? "You sicced your dog on me."

"Sicced, huh?" He made a show of looking at the deliriously happy dog, which only made her want to stomp her foot like a toddler. Daniel raised his eyebrows. "Are you feeling threatened? Because Ollie here looks pretty fucking threatening right now."

"Shut up." He didn't get to surprise her in the kitchen

with mind-blowing sex, lay claim to her vagina, and then turn around and poke fun at her. "I need space."

It was clearer than ever that this wasn't working out. She'd shown up here expecting… She didn't know what she'd been expecting. When she'd driven from Dallas, she'd been convinced he would say all the right things and then she could go back to her life, well assured that he'd be supportive in the way she envisioned. That they would be partners—long-distance partners.

Apparently that had been her delusions talking.

The truth was that Daniel wasn't the only one to blame for things going south so quickly. She was too keyed up, and it was making her emotions flip-flop faster than even she could follow. If she'd told him to back off sexually, he would have. *She* was the one who'd made the first move. So the blame for that, at least, lay firmly in her court. Hope held up a hand. "Space, Daniel. Respect it or I'm getting in my car right now."

He stopped in the middle of walking toward her. "You don't get to throw that threat around whenever it pleases you."

"Wrong. We aren't dating, and we sure as hell aren't married. I might be having your baby, but that doesn't mean *I'm* yours." She hated the way his mouth tightened with each word, but she needed to make this as cut-and-dried as she could. She'd been back in Devil's Falls all of a weekend and it was more clear than ever why they wouldn't work.

"That's where *you're* wrong, darling." He leaned against the post of his front porch, looking for all the world like he wasn't worried she'd leave. Like she was a sure thing. "You never stopped being mine."

It was too much. She'd tried so incredibly hard to let go of the past and move on, but being back here and having him make claims on her he had no business making… She couldn't do it anymore. "If I was really yours, you wouldn't have left me in that hospital alone, Daniel. You would have been there when I woke up. You would have been at my side when we buried my brother. You wouldn't have stared right through me as if I wasn't there. You would have, I don't know, returned a single phone call instead of letting me twist in the wind. I'd lost so much, and then you went and made sure that I lost *everything*."

It hurt to say, like she was traveling back in time to that terrified eighteen-year-old girl who'd woken up an only child and watched her college track scholarship disappear before her eyes. She'd clung to the fact that at least she still had Daniel…except then she didn't have him, either.

He flinched. "Darling—"

"Do *not* call me that."

They stood there, staring at each other across a distance that should be easily crossable. If only he would take the first step, if only he'd been willing to bend just a little. He wouldn't, though. Nothing had really changed.

Daniel straightened. "It was a mistake."

"I know this was a mistake."

"No, that's not what I'm saying. Back then, I made a mistake. Fuck, I made more than one. We went out that night and I knew I was the designated driver, and I still had two beers."

Her eyes went wide. *Surely he doesn't still blame himself for that?* "I don't know how things are for you now, but back then two beers wasn't even enough for you to catch a buzz."

"I blew a point-oh-nine."

"That doesn't mean you were drunk." She'd known he wasn't drunk. In all the scenarios that had played out in her head over the years, she'd always comforted herself with the knowledge that Daniel had to know that that car crash was beyond his control. "It was raining like crazy and that truck lost control. You were trying to avoid a head-on collision."

"Instead, I rolled the car, killed John, and crippled you."

She jerked back, biting down on her instinctive response to that. This moment wasn't about her. It was about him and the guilt that had been poisoning him for far too long. "No one could have done better. Everyone knows that." Everyone except, apparently, Daniel.

But he wasn't listening. He stared off into the distance. "How could I face you, Hope? We all loved John, but he was your big brother. He'd always suspected I wasn't good enough for you, and that night I proved him right."

"You're rewriting history. Don't you dare put the memory of John between us." She drew herself up. "He might have been your best friend, but he was *my* brother. He wouldn't have blamed you for the crash any more than I did. You made your intentions to marry me after I got through college pretty damn clear. He thought we were great together."

His shoulders dropped a fraction of an inch. "There's no way you don't blame me for that. It's impossible."

"Well, then pigs are flying, because I don't. I never have." She waited a beat, silently debating just letting this go. But it was like lancing a wound—it was time to get it all out there. "I blame you for abandoning me afterward."

"I couldn't face you." He shook his head. "I might not have taken off like Adam did, but it was everything I could do to go to the funeral. It was bad putting John in the ground, but it was almost worse seeing you in that chair, looking like you had one foot in the grave. I just…I thought you'd be better without me in your life."

He'd been mourning, the same way she had. The difference was that he'd only seen what he'd lost, rather than what was still left. Mainly *her*. Because of her leg, apparently. "If you couldn't handle the thought of being with a *cripple*, then just say it. It's fine—you didn't sign on for that when we started dating. But don't try to pretty it up like you were doing me a favor." Suddenly exhausted, she wobbled over to drop onto the step next to where he stood.

He sank down next to her. "I don't think you're a cripple."

"You literally just said that."

"I didn't mean it like that. I just meant…" He sighed. "I'm sorry."

"Bully for you." She didn't really want to talk about her injury. It was just another opportunity for him to wallow in decade-old guilt instead of focusing on the current issues. "My point, which we've stampeded away from, is that you are the one who ended us. Not me. So you don't get to just decide that you're picking back up where we left off. That's not how it works."

"Do you still love me, darling?"

Her breath stilled in her lungs, and her eyes went wide. The world tilted crazily around her like it had last time she had the misfortune of being on a carnival ride. She hadn't liked the experience any more then than she did now. "*What the hell kind of question is that?*"

His smile was the very definition of smug. "I thought so."

God, the man was just infuriating. She threw up her hands, torn between strangling him and strangling *herself.* "Have you been listening to a single thing I've been saying?"

"Yeah. I did you wrong—in more than one way. I know I can't make up for that shit, or ever really lay it to rest because it's always going to occupy space between us, but I can start by doing right by you from here on out."

He kept saying that. *Do right by you.* It was like he thought this baby represented a chance to balance out his karmic debt. Which was all well and good for him, but she wasn't a debt and she didn't want to be with a man who saw her as his burden to bear. "I swear to God, if you propose to me, I'm going to punch you in the face."

Daniel stood and offered her his hand. "I lose my head

around you. What we had…it was a once-in-a-lifetime kind of thing. So forgive the fuck out of me if I'm more than willing to play dirty to get you to stay. I know I'm screwing up, but I'm trying my damnedest."

All she wanted to do was walk away. It *hurt* being with him, like a knife twisting in her stomach over and over again. But there was more than her to think about now. It didn't matter how complicated their history was—her baby would know his or her father. *Daniel will be a good father.* She'd always known that, and apparently she was going to get a chance to see it in real time.

Hope inhaled deeply and took his hand. "Tone down the possessive crap—starting now."

"I'll try."

It wasn't much of a promise, but it wasn't like she was an innocent in this, either. She'd known things between them were too intense, full of too much potential to blow up in her face, and she'd still had sex with him. More than once.

Truth be told, she kind of wanted to go there again.

And, damn it, he knew. Daniel's smile made her stomach do a slow flip. "You've got that look in your eye, darling. I've been an asshole. Let me make it up to you."

Even though she knew better, she followed him back into the house. "You've set a pretty high bar for yourself if you're going to try to fix every fight we have with sex."

"Believe me—I'm more than up for the challenge."

Chapter Ten

Hope kept a hold of Daniel as he led her into his bedroom, feeling like she was in the middle of the storm and he was the only thing keeping her from being swept away. Ironic, since *he* was the one responsible for the storm in the first place. But with him looking over his shoulder at her with those dark eyes, and his calluses rubbing against the palm of her hand, she couldn't think of a good reason to put a stop to this once and for all.

It's too late. There's no stopping it now, no matter what I do.

She touched her stomach with her free hand, wondering how so much could have changed and yet nothing at all. They'd barely crossed the threshold when he swept her into his arms. In the back of her mind, she knew it was because he wanted her to be careful with her knee, but her pride had nothing on the feeling of being this close to him. *This is really happening.* She couldn't blame this on hormones getting the better of her, or on an impulse she had too little self-control to resist.

She was making the choice to have sex with Daniel Rodriguez.

He set her on her feet and stripped her shirt off. She could barely comprehend the way he looked at her, like he'd never seen anything so beautiful in his life. *He used to look at you like that.* Yeah, *before.* She closed her eyes and tipped her head back, silently demanding a kiss he seemed all too ready to deliver. His hands sifted through her hair to cup the back of her head and his lips brushed against hers, teasing her mouth open. She opened for him. She was helpless to do anything else.

His skin was so damn warm beneath her hands. She cautiously slid them up his sides to his chest, not pushing him away, not pulling him closer, just relishing the ability to touch him to her heart's delight. Daniel made a sound that was damn near a growl at her nails dragging over his skin, so she did it again.

"We'll go slow this time."

She barely had a chance to register the words when he toppled them back onto the bed, twisting just enough that she didn't take his full weight. She could have told him it didn't matter. She wanted everything he could give her, wanted to lose herself in the feel of him, wanted to just stop thinking for one fucking second and enjoy this.

Of course, he knew. He always knew. Daniel shifted to kiss along her jaw. "Turn off that beautiful brain of yours, darling. We'll figure it out. I promise. But right now I'm more concerned with getting you out of these pants."

Fear, cold and irrational, rose to close her throat. Taking off her pants meant baring her scar to him and being forced to witness that horrible guilt on his face. Then she wouldn't be the only person thinking too much. She opened her mouth, but no words came out.

He kissed her again, his hands going to the waistband of

her pants and underwear, and she lifted her hips to allow him to slide them down her legs. His movement hitched when his fingers made contact with the top of her scar, but it was such a small hesitation, she wouldn't have noticed it if every fiber of her being wasn't focused on him. Daniel tossed the clothing aside, quickly followed by her bra. "Tell me about the tattoo. An anchor."

"Its whole purpose is to remain in place, no matter how strong the currents or how fierce the storm."

As usual, his dark eyes saw too much. "You always were strong, darling."

She didn't feel the least bit strong right now. She hadn't since she walked back into his life. She felt like a leaf being thrown around by the wind, free-falling in one direction and then tossed to the side, then falling all over again until she wasn't sure which way was up and which way was down. But she didn't want to talk about that right now. She didn't want to talk about anything. "Kiss me, Danny."

He did. He just didn't kiss her lips.

Daniel pressed a kiss to one hip bone and then the other, shifting to settle between her thighs. One big hand pressed lightly down on her lower stomach, and he met her gaze. There was so much left unsaid between them, but now wasn't the time. He drew his tongue over her center, a long, savoring lick that made her squirm. He kept her pinned in place, though, the feeling only heightening the sensation of pleasure as he licked her again. "You always were my favorite flavor."

I don't know what to say to that.

He circled her clit with his tongue, taking away the need to say anything at all. She reached over her head and grabbed the bottom of the headboard, needing something solid to hang onto while he drove her relentlessly to oblivion. Daniel never quite let her take the final plunge, though. He teased her, drawing ever closer to the edge, and then gentling his touches to prevent her from coming.

The third time, she cried out in frustration. "You are a horrible man."

"Mmm-hmm." He pushed a finger into her, the shock of penetration making her eyes fly open. "And you're almost ready for me, darling."

Almost ready for... She lifted her head. "Then stop teasing me and get up here."

"When you put it like that..." He crawled up her body and settled between her legs. A wild thought rolled over her that they'd been in this exact position too many times to count when they were teenagers in the back of his truck. She pressed her lips together to keep the hysterical giggle inside. Daniel raised his eyebrows. "What?"

"I feel like an idiot teenager again."

He went still, and she kicked herself for saying anything to bring them back to those days. To *that* day. But it was something that would come up again and again. If they didn't find a way to work through it, they were destined for a future filled to the brim with misery and fights and just plain awful times. *We* have *to figure it out before the baby gets here or he or she will be visiting him every other weekend like Jessica's parents forced her to do.* The thought beat back the desire coursing through her body, her mind kicking into high gear again.

Daniel shook his head. "Later."

His cock notched in her entrance and then he was inside her again, that slow, sensuous slide filling her and making her feel whole. She locked her ankles at the small of his back, allowing him that extra depth that made her back arch. "*Danny.*"

"I've missed the way you say my name when I'm inside you." He rolled his hips, sliding one arm beneath her back to seal them as close as two people could be. His lips brushed her ear with each word, sending shivers through her body in time with his short thrusts. He kissed her, and that was all it took. She clung to him as she came, her entire world narrowing down to the feeling of Daniel on top of her, beneath her, inside her. His cock filling her, his taste in her mouth.

She came down from her orgasm to realize he was still hard inside her. Hope blinked at him, and Daniel gave her a grin that made her heart skip a beat. "I set a high bar, remember?"

She didn't remember much of anything right now.

He pushed off her, adjusting their angle until her ankles were propped on his shoulders and he was on his knees. The new position nearly made her eyes roll back in her head, his cock impossibly deep inside her. He thrust, pulling out of her almost all the way and slamming home, drawing a cry from her mouth. Daniel eyed her, adjusted his angle, and did it again.

"*Oh my God.*" There was nothing to do but hang onto the headboard, riding out the waves of pleasure radiating through her.

She was vaguely aware of his strokes becoming irregular and hurried and him growling her name as he came, but she was too busy floating on a cloud of bliss to do much more than unclench her hands from the headboard and reach up to stroke them down his back where he'd collapsed on top of her. She pressed a kiss to his shoulder. "Okay, maybe you *can* fix most problems with sex."

At least temporarily.

• • •

Daniel managed to scrounge up a snack for them—a bag of Goldfish from behind the absurd number of cream of mushroom cans he'd rage-purchased earlier—but he wasn't about to let Hope out of his bed any time soon. The sex had been… Fuck, he didn't have words for how good it had been. All he knew was that the second they left this room, they were going to have to figure some shit out, and he flat out wasn't ready. This was a much-needed reprieve, and he was going to hold onto it for as long as he could.

On the other hand, there were things they needed to figure out sooner rather than later.

In all the chaos since Hope showed up again that first time, Daniel hadn't seen much of either his friends or family. Truth be told, that wasn't as abnormal as it once might have been, but he couldn't hide her away indefinitely. A weekend, yes. Any longer and word would get out—had *already* gotten out that she was back in town if the half a dozen missed calls from his mother were any indication.

He needed to let people know about the baby, but telling each person individually and having to deal with the variety of reactions that would no doubt range from shocked to pissed to joyful was exhausting to even think about. It would be easier to get them all together and deliver the news at once—like ripping off a Band-Aid.

First, though, he needed to get Hope on board. He'd already fucked things up enough without springing this on her, too. But if he could do both with one fell swoop…

He stretched, half rolling over to run a hand down her side. *Fuck, she's so beautiful, it kills me.* "I was thinking."

"Always a dangerous prospect." She opened one eye. "Go on."

"We have to tell my family eventually—and Adam and Quinn."

Hope sighed and rolled onto her stomach to bury her face in the pillow. "Can't we just tell them in approximately eight months when the baby is here? It's not like they're going to see me much in the meantime to ask why I suddenly look like a human-shaped elephant."

Eight months. It seemed like an eternity and not nearly long enough to get used to the idea of being a dad. And she was still planning on leaving in the morning. He forced himself to focus. "You know that's not an option."

"I don't see why not."

Daniel considered how to respond, trying to keep from steamrolling her like she kept accusing him of doing. "What do you say to getting together for a dinner and announcing it there? Let everyone know at once so there aren't any hurt feelings that we told one person before another."

"I suppose that would require me to make yet another trip to Devil's Falls?"

Not if she didn't leave in the first place. He ran a hand down her spine, splaying his fingers across the small of her back. "Or maybe you could take some vacation days and we could do it this week. Get it all out of the way at once." The longer she was here, the better chance he had of convincing her to stay for good.

She lifted her head. "You won't let it go, will you?"

"This is sheer self-defense." He kept touching her, trying to soothe away the tension that had bled into her muscles. "If you're there and so is the rest of my family, there's the added bonus that with everyone together, we're less likely to get new asses ripped by my parents."

Hope made a face. "Speaking of parents, I suppose we should extend an invitation to mine, too, if we're going forward with this insanity."

He bit back a denial. She was agreeing to his plan, which meant he couldn't do a damn thing to jeopardize it. He hadn't seen the Moores since John's funeral, but he couldn't get the condemnation on Mrs. Moore's face out of his head. It was one of the contributing factors that pushed him to leave Hope alone for good, though he'd never tell her that. The decision had been his, and he didn't like the idea of causing problems with her and her parents.

That didn't mean he was all that eager to see them again.

But he'd fake it. For Hope. He cleared his throat. "That sounds great."

"Liar." She laughed softly. "But if we're going down together, it might as well be in flames."

Daniel kept stroking her back. "We can do this, darling. I promise." It struck him that he'd made promises to her before, a lifetime ago, and he'd failed at following through on a single one of them. Promises that he loved her, that they'd have a future together, that he'd be by her side through thick and thin.

I fucked up before. I won't do it again.

"Don't make promises you know you can't keep." She blinked at him from beneath a tangle of blond hair, as pretty as a picture, made all the more attractive because it was because of *him* that her lips looked so kissably plumped and *his* whiskers that left light marks on her pale skin. He felt out of control and damn near animalistic with the need to mark her, to prove to anyone who came too close that she was his and his alone. It didn't matter that he didn't have a right to claim her.

He'd given up being an honorable man a long time ago.

"We'll talk about it later…but later isn't here yet." She rolled into him, hooking his neck and pulling him down to her. "Now, kiss me and let's stop worrying for a little while."

Chapter Eleven

"It's been a minute, stranger."

Daniel kept his cell to his ear as he closed the door to the truck, doing his damnedest to ignore the censure in his friend's tone. "I've been busy."

When Hope had woken up, she'd developed a totally bizarre craving for Greek yogurt, so he was hustling to pick some up before she starved to death since that was the one thing they hadn't purchased yesterday. *Pregnancy sure makes her dramatic.* Not that he'd ever tell her that to her face. Things were finally starting to actually move forward between them, and he wasn't about to do anything to fuck that up.

Not on purpose.

He'd already more than proven he could—and would— fuck up on accident.

Hence, making this call while he was alone.

"Busy." Adam didn't sound all that impressed, and he shouldn't be. As far as excuses went, it was a shitty one. "By busy, I take that you mean you've been shacking up with Hope Moore for the weekend."

This goddamn town was out of control. They'd left the house together exactly one time, and that was all it took for gossip to spread like wildfire to everyone who'd listen—which was the entire population. He checked the sidewalk in front of the store, but thankfully he didn't see any of the older folk lurking, waiting to ambush him for news. If he hurried, he could get in and get out without running into someone he knew. "Word gets around."

"Yeah, well, you can't take her to Main Street and expect it not to—though I'm kind of thinking you damn well knew that." Adam didn't bother to give him a chance to respond. "What the fuck are you doing? I know things got carried away back at your birthday party, but I was under the impression she went back to Dallas."

"She did."

A beat of silence, then another. "Right, well, you don't have to confide in me about shit. But that doesn't mean I'm going to be giddy as fuck over you shutting me out—again."

Damn it, Adam had a point. He was the one who'd opened up a little over a year ago when he finally decided to stay in town for good. Daniel headed into the store, keeping his gaze focused on the ground and his hat tucked low. The truth was, there was a reason he'd called Adam instead of just issuing a blanket invite.

He needed someone to talk to.

It was hard to force the words out, hard to make it *real* by telling someone other than himself and Hope. He scanned the store, but there was only Jessica popping gum at the register, her attention trained her phone. Still, it couldn't hurt to move deeper into the place. "She's pregnant."

Adam didn't say anything while Daniel grabbed a basket to throw the yogurt into, and by the time he'd turned down an aisle at random, he still hadn't said anything. "I'm taking that to mean you don't approve."

"What the *fuck* are you doing?"

He winced and held his phone a little farther from his ear. He surveyed the food lining the shelf in front of him. Cereal. He could do better than cereal. She would need vitamins and shit to help the baby grow healthy. *Oatmeal is better.* He frowned at the selection and finally grabbed one of the high-fiber ones. *Babies need fiber, right?* "I'm doing right by her, Adam. It's time."

"There's nothing wrong with doing right by her, but this is a fucked-up situation, and if you don't see that, you're even more fucked in the head than I thought."

Daniel narrowed his eyes, moving to the next aisle. "Tell me how you really feel." He realized he was staring at a vat of olive oil and kept going, heading for the produce section. Devil's Falls wasn't exactly a hub of all things grocery related, but surely he could find something that would sound good to Hope.

Adam seemed to realize he was being a jackass, because he took a harsh breath. "I'm sorry. But what the hell are you two going to do?"

That was the question of the hour. He knew what the ideal situation would be, but he also knew that there was no way Hope would agree to marry him just because a baby came along. Convincing her that it *wasn't* just about the baby was going to be harder than hell...but maybe that wasn't a bad thing. As she'd pointed out time and time again, what happened thirteen years ago wasn't a good enough reason to make a decision about things happening right now. Maybe it was time he finally started listening.

He picked up an apple, frowned, and set it down again. *Maybe I should make a run in to Pecos.* "She's mine, Adam. She always has been."

"If that's the case, you've done a shitty job of taking care of what's yours."

It was the truth, and that only made it sting all the more. He glared at the oranges. None of them were good enough. "I'm looking to change that now." He grabbed a cluster of bananas and set them in his basket, balancing the phone against his ear. It was time to get to the point of this call and hang up so he could focus on what food would be the best bet for Hope. "We're putting together a dinner this weekend to tell the family—both families—and I'd like you and Jules to be there."

Adam sighed. "It's going to be a train wreck."

"Probably." *Most definitely.* There wasn't an outcome where the Moores were happy about this, and he didn't think his parents would be too keen, either. They loved Hope, and he'd broken his mother's heart when he and Hope broke up, but he figured this wasn't how they dreamed they'd end up with grandchildren.

"I'll be there—for this and for whatever either one of you need down the road." He hesitated. "Don't fuck this up, Daniel. Hope's a good girl—always has been—but she's been through a lot. It hasn't broken her yet, but it's just plain cruel to pursue this if it isn't what you really want."

"I want it." He'd had a hell of a time convincing her to let him have this much. He wasn't about to jeopardize his chance to make amends by pushing her too hard, too fast.

Maybe you should have thought of that before you fucked with her car.

Daniel didn't know if he believed in karma, but if it existed, it was practically waving a flashing neon sign in his face telling him that he couldn't ignore Hope and their baby. "I'll let you know about dinner once we have the day and time finalized."

"Sounds good. And Daniel?"

"Yeah?"

"Congrats."

He hung up, a slow smile spreading across his face. That had gone better than he'd anticipated. He knew Adam wasn't happy with how shit had played out recently. Hell, Quinn wasn't happy, either, but Quinn was less likely to corner him and confront him about it. They'd worked together too long for him to rock the boat unless he thought the situation was dire. Adam didn't have that problem and, combined with Daniel's meddling cousin rubbing off on her now husband, he could be a real pain in the ass sometimes.

But all that was going to change.

Everything was going to change.

He headed for the refrigerated section, determined not to forget yogurt after he'd come here specifically for it. He laughed softly at the pile of food in his basket. *Should have gotten a cart.* Daniel stopped in front of the yogurt section. Where the store was sparse in selection in other places, someone who stocked it *really* liked yogurt. There were at least twenty different varieties. Once he found the Greek version, that narrowed his choices down to six. He frowned. Short of calling Hope, there was no telling which flavor she wanted—or if that would be the same flavor she'd want tomorrow.

Better get them all.

He grabbed as many as could fit into the basket and then had a moment of considering if he should go back and get an actual cart so he could buy more. There had to be some kind of limit on how much yogurt one woman could eat, right? He studied the basket. "Well, hell. If she wants more, I'll just come buy out the rest of the selection." Simple.

Daniel couldn't stop the stupid grin from spreading across his face at the incredulous expression Jessica gave him as she rang him up. Let her wonder what he was up to. Let the whole damn town wonder. Hope Moore was in his house and in his bed, and she was staying—without a fight—for at least a few days more.

Things are finally starting to look up.

• • •

Hope stood in the kitchen, looking at the neat rows of Greek yogurt in the fridge. She'd laughed when Daniel came back with bags upon bags of it yesterday, but it was all she wanted to eat right now. He was trying so hard and, despite her, he was starting to win her over. They hadn't really solved anything with their fight, but maybe it was better to just focus on the future instead of the injuries they'd dealt each other in the past.

She was so damn tired of fighting.

She'd delegated the two projects she'd just taken on, and she was trying very hard not to look into the fact that the two ladies who worked with her were so freaking surprised that she'd taken vacation. It was the first time in years, but *still*.

Five days. That was it. After the party, she'd go back to Dallas and that would be that.

Strawberry sounded particularly delicious this morning, so she grabbed that container and sat down on the single bar stool to eat. Three days in Devil's Falls, and she was getting twitchy. She needed a good, long workout. Hope twisted to rub her leg. Running had been her outlet once upon a time, but that stopped being an option when she was eighteen. Now she used specific exercises and yoga to keep her knee from giving her too much grief—two things she hadn't been doing since she showed up on Daniel's doorstep.

She was pushing herself too hard, and she knew it—she'd had more than enough experience over the last decade to know her limits, and she was toeing the line. If she wasn't careful, she'd have a whole lot in the way of sleepless nights in the future. The pain pills she kept as a last resort weren't an option now that she was pregnant.

God, she hated those pills. They were like the physical representation of her weakness, a constant reminder that she wasn't normal and never would be. Normal people didn't have to worry about a body part inside her skin that didn't originate with her, or about nerves that sometimes felt like they were on fire.

The problem was that Daniel had been working really hard not to pay too much attention to her leg, and she didn't want to make him uncomfortable...

Hope straightened. "What the hell is wrong with me?" She was *not* doing this again. She'd put other people first for far too long, and he was the one who kept telling her he wanted to do right by her. Her scars were part of her, and if he couldn't handle that, he had no business trying to elbow his way into her life.

She finished off her yogurt, dropped the container in the trash, and put the spoon in the sink. She'd deal with whatever work things had popped up overnight and then she'd take a relaxing bath. After that, she'd settle in with some tea and a few movies and see if a day off her feet helped. She kind of suspected it wouldn't, but she had to try.

Things were going great right up until she leveraged herself into the bath filled to the brim with bubbles...and heard the front door open. Hope shot a panicked glance at the unlocked bathroom door, but if the heavy footfalls heading in her direction were any indication, she didn't have enough time to fight her way to her feet and hope that she managed to get to the lock before the person in the hallway got to the door.

As soon as the thought crossed her mind, the door opened and Daniel poked his head in. "Hope? I'm just..." He trailed off, his gaze raking over her. "Well, fuck."

She wasn't sure what she should be trying to cover, so she didn't cover anything. Her mangled knee clearly showed over the top of the bubbles, and there wasn't a damn thing she could do about it without curling into a ball. *He has to deal with it eventually.* "Did you need something?"

"Yeah, darling. I'm starting to think I do." He stepped into the bathroom and closed the door behind him. "You usually take baths in the middle of the day?"

The question seemed innocent enough, though there was nothing innocent about the way he was looking at her. She lifted her chin. "Only when my knee is giving me grief." It wasn't strictly true. Normally, she listened to her body and avoided pushing it far enough that it knocked her on her ass. It was a rookie mistake, and she was paying the price now.

His attention focused there, his eyebrows coming together. "It's giving you grief?"

Talking about it was strange. The only person she felt comfortable being completely frank with was her doctor. Her parents did their best to be supportive, but it was easier for them to ignore her injury and pretend it didn't exist, which she was more than happy to play along with. Better for them to look at her like she'd never changed than for them to pity her. The guilt was even worse. She loathed guilt.

Hope braced herself for Daniel's reaction. "It does more often than not, but it's been worse than normal lately."

"Why?"

She hesitated, but honesty had to be the name of the game when it came to her interactions with him. To do anything else was to cheat them both. "Because I've been kind of sucking at self-care lately—though, to be fair, it's totally possible that hormones have something to do with it, too." *That's going to make things more complicated*, she realized. Pregnancy meant a big weight change, and even completely able-bodied women got clumsy. She was going to be doubly so because of her bum knee.

Hope sank into the water up to her chin, battling the

overwhelming stress trying to take over. The whole reason she'd wanted this bath to begin with was to destress, and now it was looking like the opposite was going to be true. It was her own fault. She should have put the brakes on things until she considered all that was going to change. She hadn't. Taking it out on Daniel might make her feel better in the short term, but it wouldn't last.

And it wasn't fair to him.

"You haven't been taking care of yourself because of me," he said. She half expected him to launch in to some self-recrimination—to, God forbid, to start blaming himself for that in addition to everything else *again*. Hope took a deep breath, ready to tell him—again—that this wasn't any more his fault than her brother's death was. That he wasn't a modern-day Atlas who could balance the entire world on his shoulders indefinitely.

But he surprised her and sank onto the closed toilet. "What can I do?"

She blinked, having prepared her response to how she thought he was going to react. It took her a second to catch up to reality. "Uh, what?"

"There's got to be something I can do. This is partly because you've been dancing around my emotions, and that's not fair to you." He gave her a look like he was fully aware of what she'd expected. "So what can I do to help?"

What she really needed was a massage and some of the dreaded pain pills, but neither was on the menu. "It's okay." He'd had his hands and mouth all over her body, but there was something about him touching *that* part of her that made her balk. It was too much, even more personal than having sex. She couldn't ask that of him. "I'm really okay."

He opened his mouth like he wanted to argue with her but finally nodded. "If you change your mind, I'm here. If you don't, that's okay, too." He pushed to his feet. "Do you need anything right now?"

It was difficult to wrap her mind around this accommodating version of Daniel. *He's trying to keep this peace going as hard as I am.* She didn't really need anything, but she'd already shut him down once and he obviously needed to feel like he was helping with something, so she said, "Maybe a glass of water?"

"Sure." He looked relieved. Daniel disappeared, coming back a few minutes later with a tall glass of ice water. He set it carefully on the edge of the tub but didn't immediately straighten. Instead, his gaze rested on the bubbles partially hiding her from him. "One more thing before I go."

She barely had a second to process his intent before he slipped a hand into the bathtub, sliding down her stomach to stroke her between her legs. She went ramrod straight, but she wasn't sure if it was in protest or because—*oh, God*—he pushed two fingers into her. "Danny—"

"Close your eyes, darling. Let me give you this if you won't take anything else from me."

She didn't fight his order. She didn't even try. She wanted this too much to push him away, even though distance was the only thing that would save her heart in the long run. *Liar.* The truth was that her heart had always been compromised when it came to Daniel Rodriguez. Hope spread her legs as much as she could in the tub, giving him access to everything. Just plain giving him everything.

He rewarded her by picking up his pace, stroking her just like she loved, already gathering an orgasm around her, her nerve endings sparking with pleasure. She'd never met a man who knew her body like Daniel did, and the years apart hadn't damaged his memory any. She hissed out a breath, the sound closer to a moan than an exhale. "Danny, I'm close."

"I know, darling." His lips touched hers, a soft, sweet kiss that was completely out of sorts with what his hand was doing between her legs. The innocence of that kiss pushed her into an orgasm that locked up her muscles and drew a cry from her throat. He ate the sound, his tongue sliding against hers as he gentled his touch and brought her back to earth.

It was only when she stopped shaking that he rested his forehead against hers for a long moment and retrieved his hand from the water. His shirt was soaked, but his slow smile said it was worth it. Daniel pushed to his feet. "I'll see you this evening." And then he was gone, leaving her wondering what the hell just happened.

Guess he wasn't joking about fixing everything with sex.

The problem was, as good as being with him felt right now, she couldn't shake the feeling that they were only administering a Band-Aid instead of actually *fixing* anything.

Chapter Twelve

By the time the dinner rolled around on Friday, Hope was a hot mess. She'd changed for the third time and was going back for a fourth when Daniel intercepted her. "You look great."

"I feel like a…" She pulled at her sundress. Surely it hadn't been this tight last time she'd worn it? She felt like she was walking around with a giant scarlet *A* on her chest, that anyone who looked at her would know that she was pregnant with Daniel's child and that it hadn't been planned. "I don't know. Something huge and ungainly."

He raised his eyebrows. "You're seven weeks along, darling. You haven't changed a bit."

He might not think so, but she *felt* different. The nausea that everyone seemed to talk about hadn't overwhelmed her apart from a few food aversions, but her body was just off. The food she usually loved she didn't even want in the house, and her skin felt too tight. And that wasn't even bringing up the fact that apparently naps were the name of the game right now. It was just so *wrong*.

All she wanted to do was to wrap a blanket around herself

and curl up with Ollie on the couch so she could get back her to *Gilmore Girls* binge session while she worked on what she could swing remotely, but she had to put on real clothes and leave the house and face what felt like half of Devil's Falls.

No one was going to be happy about this turn of events.

She'd very carefully not thought about what her parents would think. They were shocked she was back in Devil's Falls, but they'd accepted her excuse of needing to hammer out some last-minute details with the town board about John's scholarship. The only thing getting them to make the drive north to town was her presence here. It had been six weeks since she saw them last, and she'd been battling the guilt of how things fell out with Daniel and their hookup. It made her sick to think about facing them now. *They're going to be so disappointed in me.*

"It will be okay." Daniel turned her around to face him and framed her face with his hands. "I promise."

"There you go again, promising things you can't fulfill." And she was being depressing as all get-out. Hope took a deep breath. "I'm as ready as I'm going to be."

He searched her face and finally nodded. "Let's go, then."

The trip into town took far too little time. They'd rented the back room of the Finer Diner to give them a little bit of privacy and to make sure no one had home court advantage. *We planned this out like we're going to battle.* It felt a whole lot like waging a war rather than what should have been a joyful occasion. In another life, it might have been…

No use thinking that way. This is your life. Not that nice little land of what-if.

Daniel's parents had beaten them there. His mom rose. She was a slightly overweight Hispanic woman with the kindest eyes Hope had ever seen, who always seemed to have a giant smile on her face. That was no different now, as she rushed around the corner to hug her. "As I live and breathe! Hope

Moore!" She swept Hope up into a hug. Almost immediately, she gripped her shoulders and stepped back. "Let me look at you. Good lord, girl, but you're even more beautiful now than you were at eighteen." She registered the scar peeking out of the bottom of Hope's sundress, but her expression didn't so much as flicker. "I hear that you're running your own business. I always knew you were ambitious. Makes me so proud."

While she'd been chatting, Daniel's father had come to stand next to them. "Lori, you're manhandling her." He'd always seemed more biker than rancher to Hope, with his burly build and long graying hair and beard, but the fierce exterior was matched by an equally fierce love of his family. He hugged her, too, lifting her off her feet. "We missed you, Hope."

"I missed you, too." Against all reason, her eyes pricked, and she sniffed. She'd forgotten how much she loved the Rodriguezes—and how much they adored her.

Rodger set her back on her feet. "I hear you've decided to give our boy another shot." He gave Daniel a significant look. "It's a shame it took this long for him to pull his head out of his ass."

"For God's sake, Dad." Daniel crossed his arms over his chest. "You know there were extenuating circumstances."

Extenuating circumstances like him blaming himself for her brother's death and wallowing in his guilt.

Lori wiped her eyes, still beaming like it was Christmas morning. "None of that matters now that you're back."

I don't know if I'm back. She couldn't force the words out. Every time she said them, they felt more and more like a lie. She *wanted* to be back. But every time she was in danger of falling completely under the spell Daniel and Devil's Falls wove, something would happen to jar her back to stark reality. She wanted to believe. She just couldn't help waiting for the other shoe to drop.

Hope was saved from answering by the arrival of Jules and Adam. He didn't look particularly happy, but then, he hadn't every time she'd seen him recently. Jules, on the other hand, was grinning, just like her aunt. "Hope!"

They went through another round of welcomes, and then another when Quinn and his girlfriend, Aubry, showed up. Apparently she was Jules's best friend or something. The energy of the room was great, everyone smiling and chatting.

Which was when Hope's parents showed up.

They stopped just inside the doorway, their faces expressionless. Just like that, she knew exactly how things were going to go down. There would be no happiness here. No joy. Nothing but more guilt, filling up the room until she was liable to choke on it. She broke away from talking with Quinn and crossed to meet them, her heart in her throat. "Mom. Dad. I'm glad you're here." She wasn't, though. She kind of wished she'd saved this news to be shared privately, so it wouldn't tarnish the Rodriguez family's happiness.

"What's going on?" Her dad put his arm around her mom's shoulders, as if she would break apart if he didn't hold her tightly enough. Ever since Hope graduated, her mom had become almost…brittle. As if she'd managed to put a good face on things and hold it together until she was sure her one remaining child would be okay. It was only then that she'd fallen apart and never quite seemed to put herself back together again.

Now, in the room full of John's old friends and the Rodriguezes, she looked like she was about to burst into tears.

Hope cleared her throat. "I, uh, *we* have something to tell you."

"Oh, God, don't tell me you're pregnant."

The room fell silent, the harsh words seeming to take up physical space, creating an atmosphere that no one was willing to break. The seconds ticked by—five, ten, fifteen, twenty.

She jumped when Daniel's arm slipped around her waist, a comfort she hadn't been aware she needed until it was there. His expression gave nothing away, but his dark eyes weren't happy. "Yes, you're going to be grandparents."

Hope's mother swayed like she might faint. She pinned Hope with a look. "How did this happen? You said you weren't seeing anyone, let alone *him*. You said nothing about seeing him when you were here for *John*."

She had to say something, but she couldn't push the words past her closed throat. Daniel didn't seem to have the same problem. His arm around her tightened, a slight tremor the only indication that he was as unsteady as she was. "It might not have been planned, but it doesn't matter. We're having a baby."

Her mom made a face like she was going to say something to cut straight to the bone, but her dad cut in. "I think now isn't the best time to talk about things. We all need some time and space to calm down so we can talk rationally." He nodded at Hope, pointedly not looking at Daniel. "We'll call you, honey." And then they were gone, sweeping out the door and leaving awkward silence in their wake.

Well, that's a great sign of things to come.

• • •

Daniel could feel the tension in Hope's body, even if none of it showed on her face. They'd known there was a chance the people in their lives wouldn't react positively to the news, but he'd expected reactions more like Adam's—shock and anger and then acceptance. He hadn't thought that the Moores would actually turn around and walk out the second they heard they were going to be grandparents.

He squeezed Hope's hip, trying to tell her that even if every other person turned their back on them, *he* would stand by her side no matter what. He owed that to both her and the memory of John. They shifted to take in the shocked expressions on the faces of every single person in the room. For one eternal second, no one said anything.

Then his mom moved forward, her dark eyes shining. "A baby?"

Hope gave a jerky nod. "I'm due May seventeenth." They'd calculated her due date using some internet site, but she had a doctor appointment in about a month to confirm it.

May 17. That's going to come up so fucking quick.

"Oh, honey, that's wonderful." She hugged Hope again, meeting Daniel's eyes over her shoulder. There was so much there—too much to readily decipher. It was like he'd offered his mom a lifeline in the middle of a hurricane when she'd given up hope of a rescue. It was too much for the news they were giving her. He didn't deserve that look for what had started as yet another fuckup in a long line of fuckups. Daniel might not view it that way now, but it wasn't like he and Hope had planned it out. The damn condom broke, and this was where they ended up.

Then there was no time for him to focus too closely on that, because it was hugs and congratulations and more than a few tears. The only faces not happy were Adam and Quinn, and he knew he was going to catch more than a little shit about it before too long.

It didn't matter.

He was here with the people he cared most about in the world, with the woman he'd never gotten over next to him, and the entire future laid out before them, full of possibilities.

As if the last thirteen years hadn't happened.

As if they really had a chance.

Really, he should be over the moon right now—and part of him was. The other part, though? The other part couldn't get the betrayed looks Hope's parents had given him out of his head. They'd wanted him to know he'd already done enough and he was a selfish piece of shit to be taking *this*, too. He shouldn't care. The only person who mattered was Hope. But then, Hope hadn't agreed to staying beyond this week. He'd done his damnedest not to push her, and so they hadn't talked again about her staying in Devil's Falls. For all he knew, she was still planning on heading back to Dallas.

He knew what side of the argument her parents would side with.

Growing up, the Moores had been like second parents to him. Adam's mom did her best, but she was a single mother with a little hell-raising asshole to bring up. Quinn's parents had never really approved of any of his friends, the exception maybe being John. As a result, their group split their time equally between the Moores and Daniel's parents' place. He'd never thought he'd live to see the day they looked at him like he was shit on the bottom of their shoe.

But then, he'd killed one of their kids and crippled the other.

"Are you okay?"

He blinked, finding Hope's hand on his arm, a worried look in her brown eyes. Daniel dredged up a smile from somewhere. "I should be asking you that."

"Yeah, well, it's been a hell of a day."

And it wasn't over yet. He forced a smile and mingled with his family, though they could have been speaking Greek for all he registered it. His mind kept going around and around, bouncing around like a pinball as he tried to come up with something—*anything*—to convince Hope to stay.

They ate, the food tasteless in his mouth, and as soon as it was cleared away, his mother stood. "I think that's more than enough excitement for one day. Hope, I know this wasn't planned, but never doubt for a minute that we consider you a daughter and we love both you and the baby unconditionally."

She reached over and squeezed Hope's hand. "If you need anything at all while you're here, don't hesitate to call."

"Thank you."

She sank into the seat next to him and leaned down to rest her head on his shoulder. They watched the Rodriguez clan clear out in record time. Adam nodded at him as Jules towed him through the door. *I'll be hearing from him sooner rather than later.*

Quinn and Aubry stopped in front of them. The little redhead gave Hope a considering look. "I don't really like kids. Disgusting creatures, and I'm pretty sure they were put on this earth with the sole purpose of destroying everything within reach." Quinn cleared his throat and nudged her, and she sighed. "But, as you're going to have Daniel's spawn and said spawn will be related to Jules, I'm willing to make an exception to my no-kid policy."

Hope's lips twitched. "I very much appreciate that."

"Quinn, stop nudging me. I know I'm an ass." Aubry rolled her eyes. "The man should know by now that I'm untrainable in polite society."

Daniel coughed to cover a laugh, but the chuckle broke free when Quinn cursed and tossed Aubry over his shoulder. "Peaches, we're going to have to talk about your bedside manner."

"I don't have a bedside manner."

"Exactly."

The door closed behind them, and Hope visibly slumped. "That was something else."

"Yeah." He didn't have the words he needed. Any of them. He didn't know what to say to fix this thing that had been broken between them for half their lives. He didn't know if he *could* fix it.

"I don't know about you, but I'm exhausted."

He'd been so busy brooding, he'd missed both those

important things. *Hard to convince her to stay so I can take care of her when I'm doing such a stand-up job.* "Let's get you home, then." A strange look passed over her face, and he paused. "What?"

"Nothing. It's just funny how things work out, you know?" She accepted his offered hand and let him pull her to her feet.

He knew what she meant, but he still said, "Certain things are meant to be."

Hope shot him a look. "Fate, Daniel? Really?"

"No." Fate was too broad a term, and it took away personal responsibility. He didn't believe in fate. There was no way that something like John's death and Hope's mangled leg would be preordained. That was human error of the most unforgivable nature at work. He kept hold of her hand as they walked out of the diner. "But you and me, darling? It doesn't matter if it's a day or a decade—we're going to find our way back to each other again and again until we get it right."

"I don't know if that's depressing or reassuring."

"Both." For all appearances, she'd moved on before that night when they'd lost control and put themselves on their current path. She had a life, and it was on hold until they determined if this was a second chance or just another opportunity to fall apart. Which made it doubly important that they figure out their shit once and for all this time around.

He held the door open for her, that thought circling round and round in his head as he got in the driver's seat and headed for home. He knew damn well that things weren't perfectly fine between them. There was too much unsaid, too much that *had* to remain unsaid because they didn't see eye to eye on it. He wasn't willing to fight with her over his guilt, or the fact that he'd fucked up beyond belief thirteen years ago.

So how to prove that he was truly willing to go the distance now when he'd dropped the ball so spectacularly before?

Daniel tightened his grip on the steering wheel. He didn't

know, but he was going to have to figure it out fast. Neither of them said anything until he pulled up in front of his house and shut off the engine. "I'm sorry about your parents."

"Don't be. I'm not going to pretend I'm not upset by how they took the news, but I'm hoping they'll come around. They have eight months to figure it out." She didn't sound any more hopeful than he was about it.

He got out and moved around to open her door, well aware that she sat there and let him. They were both trying so fucking hard, it was almost painful. Once upon a time, being with her had been the most natural thing in the world. He wanted to get back to that point. Tonight. Now.

Daniel maintained his hold on her hand as they crossed to the front door and walked into the house. He had to let go long enough to refill Ollie's water and food, but Hope waited in the doorway. It was almost like they both knew that this could be the turning point that either made or broke them, and neither was willing to do or say something that would fuck it up.

He knew who was most likely to be the one to push them over the edge.

Finished, he stood and took her hands. "I'm going to make love to you now."

She opened her mouth, seemed to reconsider, and shut it. Instead of saying anything, she leaned forward and delivered the single sweetest kiss of his life, one filled to the brim with innocence that he'd thought long gone and buried for both of them. There were so many fragile possibilities there that he fought to maintain the gentleness she'd used to set the tone.

It didn't use to be a fight. He'd always touched Hope like she was the most priceless thing in his life—because she had been.

She still was.

And, suddenly, it was the most natural thing in the world

to cup her face and smooth his thumbs up over her jaw and across her cheekbones. He picked her up, sweeping her into his arms in a way that made her laugh. "No laughing. This is serious business."

Her dark eyes sparkled. "Serious business, huh?"

"Fuck, no, darling. Keep laughing. I'm addicted to the sound." He laid her on his bed and propped himself up next to her, immediately returning to the soft touches he'd started with. They'd had sex recently, but it had been rough and frenetic. That wasn't what tonight was about.

Tonight was about finally putting both feet forward into the future.

He slowly undid her dress, pressing a kiss to the skin exposed by each button. Her breathing was already ragged, but he was nowhere near finished. He was going to properly reacquaint himself with her body—and drive her crazy while he did it. Daniel reached the last button and smoothed his hands down over the fabric covering her hips and thighs, knowing damn well that she'd picked an outfit that was designed to play down her scars so she didn't make anyone uncomfortable.

Well, fuck that.

He urged her up so he could finish getting off the dress and then palmed first one breast and then the other. "You're beautiful."

"You've always said that. Even when I was a gangly teenager."

He pinched her nipple lightly, relishing her harshly indrawn breath. "It was true then. It's even truer now." He peppered her breasts with light kisses designed to torment and moved down her body, licking along the edge of her panties. "The first time I realized you weren't a kid anymore was that summer when you were thirteen."

"The pool party at Quinn's." The words came out breathy,

making him grin.

"The very one. You wore that blue bikini, and I felt like a dirty old man because my cock wouldn't calm the fuck down."

Hope laughed. "You were sixteen. A stiff wind made it impossible for your cock to calm down."

He liked this, revisiting the good memories. Daniel worked her panties down her hips, stopping when they hit the tops of her thighs and she tensed. To distract her, he kept talking. "I knew John would kick my ass, so I stayed the hell away from you."

"And ended up making out with Christie Jenkins, if I remember correctly."

Now it was his turn to laugh. "Yeah, well, you had a point about my being sixteen." He kissed the sensitive skin below her belly button. "You want to know something?"

"Sure."

"That day had nothing on when I saw you at my birthday party seven weeks ago." He licked her hip bone until she squirmed. "All I wanted was to haul your ass out to my truck and bury my cock inside you."

"Didn't even make it to your truck."

He inched her panties down farther, kissing the point where thigh met hip. "Nope. And my cock hasn't calmed down since, either."

Her laugh cut off when he finished pulling her panties off, leaving her naked. He feathered his fingers across the top of the scar, forcing himself to really *look* at it for the first time since she'd walked back into his life. When his car rolled, the passenger door had caved in, impaling her leg with pieces of metal. It caused the scar to be jagged, an ever-present reminder of the trauma she'd gone through.

More importantly, the trauma she'd *survived*.

"Danny—"

"Do you trust me?"

She propped herself on her elbows, looking down her body at him. "You don't have to be at peace with my scars to have sex with me."

No, he didn't. But he'd been fucking up when it came to this injury since she walked back into his life, and he was done. Hope had hurt herself to spare him a situation where she thought he might be uncomfortable, and the thought of her doing it again... Over his fucking dead body.

But if he pushed too hard, she'd get up and walk to the bedroom she'd claimed as hers and shut the door on him and his attempt to truly start new with her.

So he met her gaze. "When I said you're beautiful, I meant every inch of you. That includes this." He stroked her thigh, down over the scar to her knee. There was nothing of her original skin there, some of it having been grafted from elsewhere during the surgery. "You're beautiful here, too."

"Danny—" His name was choked from her lips.

He stopped. "Am I hurting you?"

"No."

He still didn't take his hand away. "Do you want me to stop?"

It took her longer to respond this time. Hope shook her head. "I don't think so."

In the week she'd been back in town, he'd never heard her sound so unsure—not even when she was waving a box of pregnancy tests in his face. He kissed her thigh. "You don't have to hide this from me, darling. Not anymore." It hurt seeing it, but at the same time...it was part of her, and had been part of her for almost as long as she'd had an uninjured leg. If he couldn't accept this, he had no business pushing her to stay.

When he looked at it like that, it was really no contest. "What do you do when it's bothering you?"

"Daniel."

He stopped and met her gaze. "What do you need from me?"

"We can have this conversation later. Right now, I want your mouth and hands on me and your cock buried deep inside me."

There was no arguing with that. He didn't want to. Hearing the words—the plea—out of her lips was enough to have him once again battling for control. *You promised her you'd make love to her. Falling on her like a starving man isn't going to cut it.* He moved up to settle between her thighs. "Find something to hang on to, darling."

Chapter Thirteen

Hope couldn't breathe. She wasn't sure if it was the fact that she was in bed with Daniel, feeling more naked than she ever had, or the fact that he was going to *make love* to her, or if her hormones had finally decided to revolt and just finish her off entirely.

Probably a combination of all three.

Daniel's tongue on her clit slammed her back into the present. He kissed her there like he had every other part of her body on his journey south, like she was the most precious thing he'd ever come across. Like she was as beautiful as he kept claiming.

His hand drifted over her scar, and she tensed, but he didn't stop what he was doing with his tongue, and it took a grand total of two seconds before she was too busy trying not to squirm to worry about his fingers stroking her jagged skin. She closed her eyes, but that only made the dual sensations more prominent. Hope hissed out a breath. "Danny, you don't have to do this."

"This is part of you." He shifted, pressing a butterfly

kiss to her knee, the most mangled part of her. There was no hesitation, and when she looked down her body at him, for once there was no guilt in his eyes. Just a slow appreciation that always seemed to show up when he had her naked. He'd looked at her like that when she was eighteen and, silly her, she'd been sure that would never happen again. Apparently she'd been wrong. He kissed her calf at the bottom of the incision they'd made for the knee replacement. "I said it before, and I'll say it until our dying day—you're beautiful, inside and out. You're so damn strong, it humbles me. That car crash would have broken anyone else who went through what you did. I…" He paused, obviously struggling with the words. "You don't need my validation, but I am so fucking proud of you. And I am so damn sorry that I missed out on the last thirteen years."

He reached up and pressed his hand to her stomach just below her belly button. "I let my own head space get in the way of what needed to be done back then, and I promise I won't do it again. I'm going to be here for you and our baby every step of the way."

It was what she'd always wanted to hear from him. She wanted nothing more than to give in and relax and just believe, for one damn second, that he was telling the truth. There was no doubt he meant every word of it, but their past had left its mark on her, body and soul. She couldn't help feeling that things, even as chaotic and insane as they were, were going *too* well and that the other shoe was about to drop.

"You don't believe me." He traced a circle around her belly button with his thumb, the light touch making her shiver. "It's okay. I damaged your trust, and it's going to take time to win it back." He smiled, the expression showing one of the rare hints of the happy young man he used to be. "We have our entire lives ahead of us."

"I…" There was nothing to say. He was trying. She was

trying. Neither one of them could guarantee anything about the future or what it might look like. "Kiss me."

"You don't have to tell me twice." He crawled up to brush his lips over hers, gentle and sweet and full of things she wasn't ready to name. Except she already had, thirteen years ago. *I guess I never really stopped loving Daniel Rodriguez.* She pushed him onto his back and straddled him. It wasn't a position she could hold indefinitely, but she could hold it long enough.

Hope reached between them and gripped his cock, squeezing until he inhaled sharply. There were too many things to say, none of them right, so she didn't say anything at all. She guided him to her entrance and inside, sinking slowly, inch by inch, until he filled her completely. His hands on her hips urged her on, and she rode him, slowly, luxuriously, the building pleasure so sharp it almost hurt.

"Fuck, darling, this is as close to heaven as I'm ever going to get."

She kissed him before he could say anything else, trying to draw out the feeling of weightlessness. It was no use. Being with Daniel, having his hands on her body, was just too good. Her orgasm swept over her, stealing any worries about the future, drowning her fears, and leaving only a wonderfully sated feeling in its wake.

He flipped them, pushing deeper yet, and kissed her. He maintained that contact even as his strokes became less smooth and his grip tightened on her. It was almost like he needed her to breathe, and she couldn't shake the feeling that it was mutual. Hope clung to him as he came, a small part of her believing it couldn't possibly get better than this.

But what if it could?

Daniel collapsed next to her and pulled her against his chest. She lay staring at the ceiling, a kernel of hope taking root in her chest. There were so many reasons why this would never work, but really, they only needed one for it to actually go the distance. She turned to face Daniel and ran her hand down his chest, needing to voice the realization she'd come across earlier. "I never stopped loving you. Not really."

His eyes changed, sharpening like a wolf circling a fuzzy bunny. "I know." He continued before she could process that he'd just Han Solo–ed her ass. "I've been holding a flame for you, too. I just never thought I'd get a chance—*deserve* a chance—to be with you again."

That was the crux of the matter. He still blamed himself for everything that had happened. She wasn't idiot enough to think that seven days were enough to change that. She had a decade of therapy under her belt and sometimes she was still caught by the random thought that maybe if she hadn't had anything to drink, hadn't been so wrapped up with the promise of a full night alone with Daniel, she would have convinced them not to drive back to Devil's Falls that night. The guilt never lasted, but only because she'd had it pounded into her head time and time again that she couldn't go back and change anything. That no one in their car had done anything wrong.

That the true fault lay with the other driver, the one who had veered into their lane.

Daniel hadn't had the benefit of a neutral party telling him the same thing over and over again until he almost believed it. It would be a long, long time before she could make any headway with him—if ever. If she tried this thing with him for real, she'd have to face that. Trying to change him would only result in misery for both of them.

I hate that he's been killing himself with guilt this entire time.

He stroked her stomach, his big hand stretching from one hip to the other. "It's weird to think that there's a baby in here. Aside from you being willing to cut someone's throat for

Greek yogurt, nothing's really changed — and everything has."
The slow drag of his calluses over her sensitive skin made her
shiver. "Do you think it's a boy or a girl?"

She huffed out a laugh. "I don't know. Fifty-fifty chance."

"Yeah, I guess." A wicked glint appeared in his eyes.
"What if it's twins?"

"Daniel Rodriguez!" She covered his hand with her
own. "Why would you say such a horrible thing to me? You
remember the Conley twins? I'm pretty sure their mother
wasn't the least bit crazy before she had them, but by the time
they graduated she was about ready to commit herself just to
get some peace and quiet."

"Still." He kept up his absentminded stroking, trailing
his fingers across her stomach. "I wouldn't mind being daddy
to a little girl. I bet she'd have your get-up-and-go." A small
line appeared between his brows. "Though the thought of her
getting into the kind of trouble we got into isn't going to make
me sleep better at night."

"We weren't that bad as kids." They'd gotten into the
same mischief that most teenagers in small towns across
America did — bonfires, a little drinking, a whole lot in the
way of flirting.

Daniel kissed her temple. "No, not too bad. But it's
different when it's *our* kid."

Our kid.

She still hadn't quite wrapped her mind around that
fact, but it was nice talking like this — like they might both
be together by the time the little boy or girl had grown into
a hell-raising teenager. "I'd be more worried if the baby is a
boy. You four were the ones who got into more trouble than
I could dream up."

A cloud passed over his face, but he made a visible effort
to smile. "They did call us the Four Horsemen."

She'd forgotten about that. She shifted. "It's all happened

so fast. I'm still having a hard time wrapping my mind around the fact I'm pregnant at all, let alone that there will be a baby in May." *A baby.* She laced her fingers through Daniel's. Would the baby have his crooked grin? Her eyes? A mass of dark hair like all the Rodriguez cousins seemed to?

It doesn't matter. I'll love him or her the same.

The fierce feeling nearly took her breath away. Hope hadn't put much thought into being a mother after she and Daniel went their separate ways. It had just hurt too much to contemplate, and though she'd dated a bit over the years, she hadn't met anyone who'd really made her consider it seriously again. She'd gotten to the point where she was more or less resigned to being childless, though she was only thirty-one. But in this quiet moment, the rightness of it settled into her chest.

"I was thinking about looking for another place."

She frowned. "Why? This house is perfectly adequate." It wasn't the house they'd always dreamed of, but that didn't mean there was anything wrong with it, other than it being the obvious residence of a guy who lived alone with his dog.

"Not big enough." His voice gained a rough quality that was almost embarrassment. "Not really kid friendly, either. They start moving pretty quick from what I understand. Hard to close off any of the rooms, and the kitchen is just asking for trouble."

Not with as little as you have in it. She didn't say it, though. It wouldn't change anything, and it might damage what they had going on right now. Instead, she swallowed hard. "That's a big change."

"Seems like the time for it." He hesitated, and that was all the warning she got. "Your leg—what can I do to help?"

"I've gotten by just fine without help this whole time." The words were out and sharp enough to cut before she could think better of it.

He wasn't fazed. "There's nothing wrong with leaning on someone, darling. I know this is new enough that I don't have your trust yet, but I'm going to do my damnedest to earn it back again—and this time I won't betray it."

She wanted that. Oh, God, she wanted that future he was painting so incredibly much. She wanted her and Daniel against the world like it used to be. She wanted the low-key nights and the long days and every second they could possibly spend together.

She wanted it so much it terrified her.

So Hope just kissed him. "One day at a time, okay? I'm here. You're here. Things are working." *For now.*

But she had to make a decision in a day or two that could potentially ruin this thing between them before it got started. She was between an impossible rock and an equally impossible hard place. She could drive back to Dallas like she'd been planning—back to her life, to the job she loved, to her little apartment that she'd never found lacking until now, thinking about how empty it would be with only her in it. Or she could stay and risk everything she'd worked so damn hard for to have a second chance with a man who had dumped her like yesterday's trash when she needed him the most.

She'd forgiven him—it still hurt, but she'd worked hard to understand why he'd made the choice he had—but that didn't mean she could charge blissfully into the life he promised without a single reservation.

He heard the words she didn't speak. Daniel framed her face with one hand. "It's going to be okay—better than okay. It's going to be fucking perfect. Just you wait."

Chapter Fourteen

Daniel tipped his head back and smiled against the wind. Leaving Hope in his bed this morning hadn't been easy, but knowing she'd be there when he got home made it all worthwhile. Last night had been...perfect—more than worth the sleep deprivation caused by their staying up for hours talking and then making love again. This morning, the future stretched before him, full to the brim with possibilities he hadn't dared consider even a month ago.

It was almost too good to be true.

Or it would be, once Hope finally agreed to stay in Devil's Falls for good.

Hoofbeats coming up on his right had him turning his head to see Adam. His friend had only been back in Devil's Falls a little over a year, but he'd taken to ranching like he'd never left. Seeing him here, on the back of his horse, with his hat pulled low over his eyes, made Daniel happy.

Or maybe he was just being a fucking sap because the woman he'd never really gotten over was his again.

He slowed Rita to a trot, nodding at Adam as he did the

same. "I thought you were in the south fields today."

"Quinn and I switched." Adam shrugged. "Thought you might want to talk after how things went down last night."

It took him a full ten seconds to get his friend's meaning. Adam wasn't talking about his being with Hope—he was talking about her parents' shitty-ass reaction to the news. His hands tightened on the reins before he forced them to relax. "I didn't expect them to welcome me back into the family with open arms." The horror on their face when they realized he was the father had been hard to stomach, though. It felt like they were reaffirming everything he'd ever suspected— that they held him to blame.

That they wished he'd been the one to die instead of John.

"John's passing fucked us all up, but them most of all, I imagine. Doesn't make it okay, but it's understandable. Losing John was enough to send me into a tailspin back then, and losing my mom this year…" Adam shook himself. "If I didn't have Jules, who the fuck knows what I would have done— probably taken off again, though this time I wouldn't have come back. I can't imagine what losing a kid would be like. I hope to hell none of us ever has to go through it."

His gut twisted in on itself at the thought of something happening to the baby growing bigger inside Hope's stomach every day. He fought to keep his voice even. "I thought you weren't all that supportive of this."

"That's not what I meant when we talked before, and you damn well know it. You and Hope—back then you were as constant as the sun rising and setting each day. Seeing you looking at each other like you used to is good. My issue is if you're going through with this out of some twisted form of penance for the car crash. *That* would be fucked beyond belief."

"I love her. Always have." He didn't tell Adam that he saw this as a way to balance out some of his karmic debt, because that would just confirm his friend's worst fear. That wasn't what things with him and Hope were about—not totally. But he'd be lying if he said the thought hadn't occurred to him. A baby did not equal a brother, but at least he'd be doing something other than bringing pain and loss into her life.

"Then I'm happy for you." Adam barely waited a beat. "What are you going to do about her parents?"

That was the question, wasn't it?

It probably wasn't realistic to expect to get their blessing, but a part of him wanted it all the same. He rubbed his chin. "I guess I'm going to have to take a trip down to San Antonio at some point."

Adam's face was unreadable. "If you think that's wise." It couldn't be clearer that his friend thought the exact opposite.

"They're her parents. I'm not going to put her in a position where she feels like she has to choose one of us over the other." There was more to it than that, but he didn't think Adam would appreciate the truth. Adam's mother had always loved the hell out of him, and the entire Rodriguez family had been thrilled beyond belief when he'd married Daniel's cousin. He'd never had to deal with that push and pull that came when the parents of the woman he loved hated him.

Daniel guided Rita to the north. "It'll work out. You'll see." He sent Rita into a canter, and Adam's reply was lost in the wind of his passing. Out here, with the unending sky overhead and his horse's hooves pounding the dirt, nothing seemed impossible. All he had to do was talk to the Moores and they'd see reason. They might have every right to hate him, but no one could deny he loved Hope more than life itself.

You did thirteen years ago, and you had a hell of a way showing it back then.

He shoved the thought to the back of his mind and tipped his head back. "It'll work out."

Maybe if he said it enough times, he'd actually start to believe it.

• • •

Hope pushed ignore on her phone and set it aside. Since the disastrous dinner yesterday, her parents had called several times. She'd ignored every single one. She wasn't ready to talk to them, especially since she highly doubted they were calling to apologize for how they'd handled the news. No, they were calling to demand an explanation.

An explanation that, frankly, she didn't have.

She pressed her hand to her stomach. Two months along and she didn't feel that much different when all was said and done. She'd noticed this morning that her breasts were growing at a truly alarming rate—and were seriously sore—but there was none of the nausea or sickness that she'd always heard about. Rationally, she knew that at some point her stomach would start rounding and, even further down the road, she'd have to actually go into labor, but it seemed like a distant dream. Things going so well with her and Daniel had only added to the dreamlike quality of the situation. Half the time she was convinced that she'd never actually left Dallas and that this was all a hallucination as a result of a bad taco truck meal.

But it wasn't a dream, and she did have to come up with a real plan at some point.

Today.

"Hope?"

She turned as Daniel walked into the kitchen. He looked... Her heart picked up at the sight of him in worn jeans, a long-sleeved plaid shirt, and his cowboy hat pulled down low. He was dirty from working outside all day, but that only added to the allure. She bit her lip and leaned back against the counter. "Hey."

"If you could see the way you're looking at me."

She didn't have to. She knew. Hope crooked her finger at him, and he immediately crossed the kitchen to pull her into his arms. Daniel took off his hat and dropped it onto the counter next to her, his dark eyes searching her face. "How was your day?"

"Good." And it was the truth. Her pain was manageable, and she'd gotten quite a bit of work done on a new account despite working remotely. The only downside was the regular calls from her parents that she wasn't ready to deal with. She'd call them back eventually, but she wanted a few more days to figure out how to approach the conversation. She needed to have an actual plan in place before she spoke with them.

"I ran into town before coming home." He stepped back, keeping his hands on her hips. "Jessica says you haven't called her and if she has to drive out here and kidnap you, she's more than willing."

Hope laughed. "I'll call later, I promise." It would be good to catch up, especially now that she wasn't feeling quite so off center when it came to wondering what the hell was going on with her and Daniel. They might not have a plan, but they loved each other. It was a start—a promising start.

"I also grabbed a few things." A frown flickered over his face, gone almost as soon as it had appeared. "I figured I'd cook us some dinner tonight. How does pad Thai sound?"

She froze, searching his face. Over a week here, and the most he'd cooked was pouring cereal into a bowl or pulling a container of yogurt out of the fridge for her. "Why now?"

"It's time."

That wasn't really an explanation, but it couldn't possibly be a bad thing. Maybe it was a sign of him starting to reclaim the parts of himself that had fallen by the wayside over the last decade. Either way, she wasn't about to complain about homemade pad Thai—especially when Daniel was doing the cooking. Her stomach chose that moment to growl, and she laughed. "Why don't you jump in the shower and I'll get the groceries put away?"

"Sounds good." He kissed her lightly and headed out of the kitchen, reappearing for trip after trip of grocery bags.

Hope stood there and knew her eyes were getting larger and larger at the growing pile of food on the kitchen island. She'd thought he'd gone overboard last time, but it paled in comparison to the sheer amount of food he unloaded. He had to have bought out the entire store.

He thinks I'm staying.

I don't even know if I'm staying.

He didn't quite look at her the entire time, and she didn't know what to stay. She didn't want to make him feel awkward when he was making changes for the better, but it was just so unexpected. Once he disappeared for the final time, she waited for the shower to start to begin going through the bags.

There was enough food to feed them for weeks, but that wasn't what had her raising her eyebrows. He must have gone into El Paso before he hit the grocery store in Devil's Falls, because there was an entire selection of new cookware and saucepans and utensils. They weren't exact replicas of the ones he'd had when they were together before, but it was more than enough to cook anything she could dream up.

We're going to have to talk about this, and soon. All of this. But not tonight.

Tonight was for new possibilities and to keep riding the wave that had crested the night they'd announced the pregnancy to their families. Things were good, and she didn't want to be the one to throw a wrench into the gears until it was absolutely necessary.

By the time Daniel reappeared, wearing a different pair of jeans and forgoing a shirt completely, she had everything put away and had hand washed the various cooking gear. She smiled at him. "You got ambitious today."

"Yeah, well, I figure your cravings are only going to ramp up as time goes on. I want to be prepared for those middle-of-the-night demands."

She laughed even as her heart pounded at an alarming rate. *I can't stay…can I?* "Trust you to make late-night cravings about food rather than sex."

His slow smile made her stomach flip. "Aw, darling, I'm more than capable of meeting either—or both—needs if you want another go at the kitchen."

"Oh." She knew she was blushing furiously, but she couldn't seem to stop. It didn't make a bit of sense, either. He'd had his hands and mouth all over her body countless times in the last week, and last night, he'd massaged her injured leg while they lounged around on the couch and watched bad television in between bouts of sex. It was like having a glimpse of the life she'd always wanted, and a part of her kept whispering that it couldn't last.

Which only made her want to hold it more closely.

He circled the breakfast bar and started going through the fridge to lay out the stuff he'd need for dinner. "I've been doing a lot of thinking today."

She didn't know where this was heading, but she wasn't ready to go there. Hope slipped between him and the counter and leaned up to kiss him. "Not tonight."

His brows slanted down. "We have to talk—about a lot of things."

She knew that. Really, she did. "We will, I promise. But can we just have one last night in the dream before we have to touch back to reality?"

If anything, that seemed to set him on edge. "One talk isn't going to be the end of this, darling. It's just a talk. It's what adults do—communicate."

Except so many of their talks seemed to end with fights and her despairing at ever being able to find a happy medium with Daniel. She loved him—more than should have been possible—but if love was enough, things wouldn't have fallen out the way they did all those years ago. No, they needed a plan and the ability to hold down a conversation about the future without resorting to yelling.

Unfortunately, both those things felt nearly impossible.

She implored Daniel with her eyes. "Please. One more night?"

"We have to talk about Dallas, Hope. I know you were planning on going back tomorrow."

Her chest compressed, and she forced a smile. "Then we'll talk in the morning. First thing, I promise."

"If that's what you want."

"It is."

Tomorrow would come soon enough.

Chapter Fifteen

Daniel gave in to Hope's request without arguing, and he wasn't sorry about it. They'd had a really nice dinner and then made love again, the whole experience just cementing his determination to make this the best it could be. And that meant he had to start at the beginning. He shifted, pulling her closer against him. "I want to push that talk by about twelve hours."

"What? Why?"

"I'm going to see your parents tomorrow."

She tensed. "Why am I just hearing about it now?"

"You didn't want to talk, remember? I wouldn't have said anything at all, but I couldn't get out there today and I want you to push your plans to go back to Dallas one more day."

"I can't keep postponing leaving. I know I didn't want to talk today, but eventually we do have to come up with something resembling a realistic plan." Hope lifted her head and frowned. "I really think you visiting them is a mistake. They've been calling nonstop all day, and *I* haven't even talked to them."

"I know." And he also recognized how her mouth tightened every time she pushed ignore on her phone. She had always been close with her parents—especially her mother—and being on the outs with them was taking its toll. There were so many things in their life right now that he couldn't control, but he could take the first step in making this right. "Darling, their problem isn't with the fact that you're pregnant—it's that you're pregnant with *my* baby. There's nothing you can say that will affect their opinion—but maybe I can." He had his doubts, but the only alternative was to cut them out of his and Hope's life, and that wasn't right. They were good parents, and they'd be good grandparents. It wasn't their fault that they weren't thrilled that their son's killer was shacking up with their daughter.

He couldn't be the reason Hope lost what remained of her family.

"You don't have to do this."

"I know that, too." He guided her head back to his shoulder and smoothed his hand over her hair. "It's just one conversation. I'll be gone and back before you know it."

She sighed. "I guess my girls can hold down the fort for one more day. But that's it. No matter what happens with us, I *do* have to go back to Dallas. I know you're not going to change your mind about going to San Antonio, so do what you feel is necessary."

He hated how defeated she sounded, but her doubts were unfounded. This was going to go a long way toward fixing things. Hope might not see that because she was wrapped up in guilt over disappointing her parents and worry over the future, but he knew he was right. Daniel drifted off to sleep with that thought centered in the forefront of his mind.

He woke up alone. He blinked and stretched, his hand encountering paper. For half a second, he was convinced that Hope had slipped out of his bed and his life in the middle of the night like a thief, but then his half-awake brain processed the words she'd written.

Went for a walk before it got too hot. If you're gone before I'm back, just know I love you.

A smile fixed itself on his face and stayed there all the way through showering, dressing, and grabbing a bite to eat before he hit the road. Hope still wasn't back, so he scrawled a quick response to her on the same note and left it propped up in the kitchen next to the coffeemaker he started on his way out the door. If the last week was any indication, she'd have a single cup and then switch to decaffeinated tea, but he figured she wouldn't want to wait. And it made him feel good to know he was meeting her need before she even thought to ask.

Maybe that made him the caveman she often accused him of being, but he was okay with it.

The drive to San Antonio passed in a blur. He kept the radio cranked up and the windows cracked, but the noise didn't quite drown out the little voice inside him whispering that this was a mistake—that there wasn't an option where this encounter ended positively. He ignored it just like he had from the moment it start popping up.

Once he hit the city limits, he followed his written directions to a little suburb with houses in neat little rows and perfectly manicured front lawns. The Moores' was a understated gray with sharp white trim that fit them perfectly. He turned off his truck and stepped out, the heat of the late morning making his shirt stick to his back. Or maybe that was just nerves.

It didn't hit him until he was knocking on the front door that maybe he should have called first. Gary Moore had always worked, and though he was closing in on retirement age, Daniel kind of doubted he'd have stepped out voluntarily. He knocked before he could talk himself out of it and was rewarded a few seconds later by footsteps on the other side of the door.

Lisa Moore opened it a crack and stared at him. "What are you doing here?" She didn't sound particularly angry, but calling her tone welcoming would be a stretch of the truth to the point of lying.

He took off his hat. "I came to talk, ma'am. I figure we're due."

"You're about thirteen years too late and more than a dollar short." She took a step back and opened the door wider. "But since my daughter isn't returning my phone calls, I suppose this is going to have to do."

Not the most promising start, but he followed her deeper into the house. She led him to a small living room off the main hallway that, judging from the pristine whiteness of every piece of furniture in it, didn't see much use. Talking in the kitchen would have been a better sign, but he'd take what he could get. Daniel perched on the edge of one of the chairs, half concerned that he'd leave a dust imprint when he stood. "I love your daughter."

Lisa waved that away. "You want to have sex with my daughter. That wasn't love when she was eighteen, and it's surely not love now."

Daniel jerked back. "Excuse me?"

"I've spent considerable time wondering what I'd say to you if we ever had the misfortune of being in the same room again. After John—" Her breath caught, but she soldiered on. "After my son died, it went quite a bit differently in my head than it will go today. I blamed you, and I'm not particularly proud of that. You were all just kids, and it was easier to have a target for my grief." She sighed. "That kind of pain never quite goes away, but it fades a little, and I've worked through the worst of it. We all have."

That was better than he could have dreamed. *Too good.* He wasn't fortunate enough to show up here and find arms opened in welcome. If that were the case, they wouldn't have reacted so poorly to finding out Hope was pregnant with his baby.

He tensed, waiting for the other shoe to drop.

She didn't make him wait long. "You weren't responsible for killing my son, regardless of what my feelings were at the time." He didn't have time to process the full meaning of her words before she verbally kicked him in the face. "However, you did fail my daughter when she needed you the most."

Daniel flinched. "I thought it would be better if I made myself scarce."

"You were a coward." She said the words softly, without any anger. "Do you know how many nights Hope spent crying because you never returned her calls? No? I can tell you. Three hundred and seventy-two. She mourned her brother just like the rest of us, but John's loss wasn't what kept her up at night when the pain of her leg got too much. She never blamed you for the car crash—and even went so far as to tell me how out of line *my* anger at you was. For three hundred and seventy-two days she held on to hope that you would come to your senses and come for her. But you never did."

Daniel didn't know what to say. He knew there wasn't a single thing he could do to make this better. Hell, he'd known it was bad, but somehow hearing it from Lisa's mouth made it so much worse. He sank back into the chair, the sheer enormity of what he'd done washing over him. "She's fine."

"She tries very hard to be fine," Lisa corrected. "Most days, it's even true. She worked to get past you, but the scars never faded. Hope doesn't lean on anyone—she hasn't since she went to lean on you and you weren't there."

If words could physically wound, he'd be bleeding out on the floor. "I love her."

"Maybe you do now. Maybe you loved her then. It didn't make a difference when you were twenty-one, and forgive me if I doubt it'll make a difference now." She pinned him with a look, her dark eyes so similar to her daughter's. "From what I understand, you never sought her out. You never chased her down. You never even tried to make things right. If you had, maybe I'd feel differently, but I suspect it was a moment of weakness on my daughter's part that resulted in this pregnancy, and I simply cannot support it." She held up her hand when he would have spoken. "Let me rephrase—I support her. I support any choice she makes for herself and her baby. What I can't support now and never will is her being with you."

She smoothed down her skirt. "You've spent the last thirteen years more in love with your guilt than you were with my daughter. I have seen no evidence that that's going to change. She deserves to be put first—both her and the baby. Not to be a consolation prize because you're still trying to make right something that will never be right again. If I thought for a second you were with her for the right reasons…" Lisa shook her head. "But you aren't. We both know that to be the truth." She motioned to the door. "I think you should leave now."

Daniel walked to the door in a daze. He'd known the Moores didn't think he was good enough for Hope, but the reasoning behind it…

How could he argue with Lisa? She was right. He'd failed Hope. Hadn't Hope herself told him as much a little over a week ago? When they'd had that argument, he'd bulldozed right over it—just like he had every other indication that there were core-deep issues that they hadn't dealt with. All he'd seen was a chance to make things right once and for all— as right as they could ever be, at least.

It hadn't occurred to him that he was doing Hope yet another wrong in his determination to make things right.

• • •

"We have to go into El Paso and look at baby stuff. I don't have any of my own, so it's up to you to give me my baby fix. I hope you're okay with that."

Hope laughed. She'd been leery of calling Jessica, but she was so nervous about Daniel off talking to her parents that she'd grabbed at the distraction with both hands. Two hours later, she was so glad she did. "We don't even know if it's a boy or a girl. I'm not even sure I'm finding out." There was something magical about leaving it as a surprise.

"Not finding out? Now you're just teasing me. What is this, 1962? I have needs, woman."

"Do I get a say in this?" Headlights shone through the front window as a truck pulled off the road and started for the house. She moved to push the curtains aside. *Daniel's back.* "I have to go, but we're still on for coffee next time I'm in town, right?"

"Wild horses couldn't hold me back."

"I'm looking forward to it, too." She hung up as Ollie came tearing into the living room, barking as loud as she could. "He's home, girl."

It seemed to take forever for Daniel to shut off the truck and make his way to the front door, but that might very well have been her nerves talking. She couldn't imagine how the conversation with her parents had gone—especially since she hadn't received a call from them since this morning. This was going to either be very, very good, or very, very bad.

One look at his face as he walked through the door and she knew it was the latter. "What happened?"

He held up a hand to stop her when she would have come to him. "We need to talk."

No good conversation ever started like that. Hope wrapped her arms around herself. She felt like she was standing on the tracks, hearing the train coming, and not able to move out of danger. "What did they say to you?"

"I thought I was doing the right thing." He said it so softly, he might have been talking to himself.

She blinked. "What?"

"We laughed about fate, but part of me couldn't help thinking that maybe you coming back into my life—getting pregnant with my child—was the universe's way of balancing everything out."

She didn't have to ask what he meant. There was only one thing he could be talking about. John. Always John. She straightened. "That was a long time ago, Daniel. I thought we were starting over." *Please let us be starting over for real.*

"I was going to make things right once and for all."

He wasn't going to let it go—*any* of it. She reeled back, feeling like the entire world had shifted beneath her feet. All Hope had wanted when she found out she was pregnant was for this to finally mean that they would both just move *on*. That they'd finally put their past behind them and start fresh. That she wouldn't be the high school girlfriend whose older brother Daniel blamed himself for killing. That he wouldn't be the boyfriend she'd loved so much who had failed her so spectacularly. "I don't know how many times I have to say it. That crash wasn't your fault. I thought you understood that." She hoped. God, she hoped so much it made it hard to breathe. *Please prove me right. Please, Daniel. I'll say whatever it takes to just end this circling we can't seem to stop doing.*

He laughed, but not like anything was funny. "If our baby was a boy, I thought we should name him John."

She gripped her arms so tightly, she distantly wondered if there would be bruises tomorrow. It didn't matter. The pain was the only thing grounding her while she tried to process the insanity coming out of his mouth. "*What?*" Suddenly it all made sense. She pressed her hand to her stomach, the nausea so intense, it was a wonder she didn't throw up on the spot. "My baby is not my brother." It came out as little more than a whisper, so she said it again. "My baby is not my brother. What the hell is wrong with you?"

He frowned at her, finally seeming to see her for the first time since he got out of the truck. "What?"

Anger unlike anything she'd ever known rose, black and thick and almost enough to choke her into silence. She wouldn't let it. Some things needed to be said, no matter how painful. "This—all of this—was about penance. You never wanted me, not really. You wanted a way to assuage your guilt and prove to yourself that you were worth a damn." She took a step back and then another.

"Hope, will you just listen?" Just that. Not a denial—a plea to explain himself.

He didn't need to explain himself. She knew how this conversation was going. The guilt on his face made her want to punch something. She shook her head. "Oh my God, I'm right, aren't I?"

"I'm no good for you. I never have been. I thought I could make everything right, but I can't."

Her shoulders sagged. "You know, I spent the last thirteen years fighting against what you're saying, and believing that I was right. Now? Now I'm tired, Daniel. I am so incredibly tired. I don't know how two and two add up to seven in your head, but I don't care anymore. If you think me being married to a man who sees me as an albatross around his neck—who sees my *child* that way—is a gift, then you're crazy. I don't have it in me to fight anymore."

She took a shuddering breath, half sure that he'd break and tell her that she was wrong, that that wasn't what he meant at all, that he loved her for who she was, not for the penance she represented. But the seconds stretched into a full minute, and the full minute into three, and he didn't do anything but look at her with that damned guilt written all over his face.

"You're right. Fuck, you're right. I don't know what I was thinking." He finally moved toward the kitchen. "You can have the master bedroom tonight, but I think it's best we go our separate ways tomorrow."

This was it. It was really happening. Instead of telling her that he loved her, he was all but admitting that he loved his guilt more. Hope shook despite her best effort to maintain control over herself. She wasn't the only woman who'd been dumped by her boyfriend while pregnant with his child, but she'd never thought Daniel would do something like this—especially since he'd all but clubbed her over the head and demanded she stay in Devil's Falls and his house. *He* had been the one driving this from day one, overriding her concerns and her fears, and now he was going to turn around and repeat history?

Her throat tried to close, but she'd be damned before she cried another tear because of Daniel Rodriguez.

Hope pushed her shoulders back and her chin up, holding it together by the skin of her teeth. "I don't think that's a good idea. Excuse me." She sent a text to Jessica as she walked slowly into the spare room and packed up her seriously small number of things. She could feel Daniel's presence in the house even if she didn't see him as she made her way to the front of the house.

She paused at the door. "My child will *not* be named John, by the way, regardless of gender."

The she walked out and didn't look back, not once.

Chapter Sixteen

"Do you want me to kill him? I can most definitely kill him."

"You can't kill him because *I'm* going to kill him."

Calling Jessica had seemed like a good idea at the time, but now Hope was starting to doubt the intelligence of her plan. She hadn't been thinking—she'd just been reacting. But no matter her logic, she hadn't expected to show up at Jessica's place and find Daniel's cousin Jules. Jules looked ready to chew through the walls when she heard how things had fallen out with Daniel, and she paced around the large living room, coming up with one plan, discarding it, and coming up with an even wilder and more elaborate one. Jessica was right there with her, egging her on.

It just made Hope so damn tired.

She wrapped a knitted throw blanket around her shoulders and curled up on the couch. Maybe if she didn't move too much, the women would forget she was here and wander back to their own lives. It was a crappy plan, but today had been filled with all sorts of crappy plans. She rested her chin on her knees and sighed, just a little.

I never wanted this. I never wanted to have everything I ever dreamed of dangled in front of me and then taken away just when I finally got to the point where I actually believed it was happening.

"Hope?"

She blinked and looked up to find Jules crouched in front of her. The concern written across the other woman's face didn't make her feel the least bit better. "Yeah?"

"Is there something we can do—aside from plan for the inevitable death of my idiot cousin? You look kind of peaky, and I can't tell if it's I've-just-been-dumped peaky or oh-my-God-the-*baby* peaky."

Hope pressed her hand to her stomach, fear beating in her throat. "I…" She forced herself to take a deep breath and *think*. She didn't even have a doctor's appointment for another month. She felt like death walking, but that was 100 percent emotional. Physically she was fine. Hungry, as always, but fine. She tried for a smile and failed miserably. "I'm okay."

"You're not, but that's okay." Jules squeezed her hand and then stood. "Why don't you get some rest? If you keep sitting here while Jessica and I plot, you'll be accessory to murder and my… What would this baby be? Second cousin? First cousin once removed?"

Hope blinked. "I don't actually know."

"Minor details." Jules urged her to her feet and turned to Jessica. "Where are you putting her up?"

The feeling she had of her life spinning wildly out of control only got worse as the night went on. She hadn't had time to process, which might be a blessing, but the very last thing she wanted to do was have the meltdown she could feel threatening with witnesses present. Hope carefully extracted her hand from Jules. "If it's all the same, I'll walk myself up to the spare bedroom." She stood on wobbly legs, hating her weakness, and walked to the stairs with as much confidence as she could muster. She doubted the show did a damn thing to convince the women behind her that she wouldn't cry herself to sleep, and she knew if she looked back, they'd have sympathetic expressions on their faces.

She didn't care.

She'd spent the last thirteen years trying to keep from going under, and she'd be damned before she started now.

Except…

That thought, that deep-seated anger that she never let anyone see, had been useful when she was eighteen and had woken up to realize the world had changed in an instant. It had gotten her through the worst pain of her life, emotionally and physically, and kept her from giving in to the sorrow that made her want to curl up into a ball and cry until things went back to how they used to be. She'd been forged in the flames and come out stronger on the other side.

Except that wasn't really the truth.

The truth was she'd never stopped hurting. She'd never stopped missing John, though the grief became manageable at some point while she wasn't looking. She'd never stopped missing her ability to run marathons like she used to, to feel her body flagging and know that it was something to push through because she was *almost* there.

She'd never stopped mourning the loss of Daniel's love.

Hope stopped at the top of the stairs, pressing a hand to her chest, the truth almost sending her to her knees. She'd told him the truth when she'd said she never stopped loving him. Even now, even knowing it would never work, that their reasons for trying to make this work were the very definition of irreconcilable differences, she loved him.

That knowledge burned her rage to ash, leaving Hope, pregnant and alone, in its wake.

She made it to the bedroom and closed the door softly behind her. Somehow she managed to get to the bed and burrow beneath covers that smelled faintly of lavender and vanilla. She curled up, placing her hands on her stomach. There was no freaking change in the last few hours, but she imagined she could feel the life growing there all the same.

He's going to miss this. The sleepless nights. The morning cuddles. All the firsts. He's going to miss everything.

Maybe I shouldn't have walked away…

But all she could see was his face when he'd said they should name their baby John. Pain arrowed through her chest, and she had to press a pillow against her face to muffle the sob that escaped. This baby deserved more than to be thought of as some kind of penance. *She* deserved it, too. Was it too much to ask that he be with her because he loved her, rather than because he was punishing himself for John's death?

Apparently so.

Another sob escaped, tearing itself from her throat, quickly followed by a third. A cry rose up inside her, desperate to be voiced.

A hand touched her head, and she startled. She'd been so focused on keeping as quiet as possible that she hadn't realized someone had come into the room. She looked up, shock breaking through her meltdown. "Mom."

"Jessica called me." Her mom sat on the edge of the bed. "I always liked that girl."

Her mom was here. Which meant…

She knew everything.

Her mom smoothed back her hair, the move harking back to her childhood—and to her months in recovery. She looked down at Hope with dark eyes so similar to her own. "I'm sorry, honey. More sorry than you can know. You deserve better than this. You always have."

There was no judgment in her tone, nothing but empathy and a desire to make everything right. Just like she always had. Hope's mom was a fixer. She saw a problem and she went in with elbow grease and sheer willpower and muscled the things around her into submission. Being so helpless after the car crash had broken something in her, something she'd never quite gotten back. That didn't stop her from trying, though.

Part of Hope wanted to blame her mom for the fight with Daniel, for exposing her weakness so thoroughly, but the truth was if Daniel had really been willing to put her first, he wouldn't have broken at the first opportunity. He hadn't fought for her.

Just like he hadn't fought for her thirteen years ago.

"Why aren't I enough for him? Why does it always have to be about John, or about what he thinks he took from me? All he can focus on is the past." She clenched her teeth, but it only made her chest hurt worse to keep the words inside. So, for the first time in far too many years, she let it out. "He loves his guilt more than he loves me."

"He's not a bad man." Her mom kept up that soothing motion, smoothing her hair back.

"You don't like him." It came out too accusing, but she couldn't take the words back. "You never forgave him."

"That's my burden to bear. Not yours." Her mom's mouth tightened slightly. "It's easier to forgive something done to you than something done to someone you love—especially a child. John wasn't his fault. You know it. I know it. What he did to you…"

A crazy part of her couldn't stop from defending him. "He blames himself for John."

"He blames himself for a lot of things."

She let out a shuddering breath. It didn't ease the burning in her eyes one bit. "I don't know how to do this. I just want to shake him until he sees that he's going to miss out on the future that could have been ours because he's so focused on whipping himself for the past."

"You have to let it go."

She jerked back. "What?"

Her mom's eyes were nothing but kind. "Honey, you have this amazing ability to put your mind to something and make it into a reality. It's an asset, though sometimes I worry about your motivations." She held a hand up. "But that's neither here nor there. My point is that Daniel isn't a problem to be fixed. He's a person. You can't change him if he doesn't want to be changed."

She knew that. Of course she knew that. But it was so incredibly hard to let go of the dreams she'd allowed herself to paint for their future. Dreams where they got married, settled into that little farmhouse they'd always talked about, and had half a dozen beautiful children. "I want it—him—so badly."

"I know, honey." Her mom gathered her to her chest and hugged her tight. "But life rarely cares about what we want."

Loss made her sick to her stomach. "I don't know if I can be a single mom."

"You can do anything you set your mind to. You'll love your baby with everything you have, and that child will want for nothing." Her mom kissed the top of her head. "And if Daniel decides to be in the baby's life—"

"He will." She might not be certain of anything else, but she was certain of that. "He might not want me, but he wants our baby." And she wouldn't stand in his way, no matter how his rejection hurt. "He'll be a good daddy."

Her mother's mouth tightened. "Likely, yes. But you deserve more than a man who will be with you for a baby. You deserve to be with a man who puts you first. And Daniel never will."

No, he wouldn't. Not when he could put his grief and guilt before all others.

Tonight. She'd give herself tonight to mourn the life she'd never have. And then, tomorrow, she'd wake up and get back to facing down the world. Dallas seemed cold after being in

Devil's Falls, so maybe she'd look into moving a bit closer—to San Antonio to be closer to her parents. Staying where she had minimal support system just to prove a point was sheer idiocy.

Hope opened her eyes, staring out the bedroom window to where the stars winked at her. "I'm going to be okay." Every other time she'd said those words, they felt like a promise.

Right now they felt like a lie.

• • •

"Well, you've gone and fucked things up beyond repair, haven't you?"

Daniel had never hated living in a small town as much as he did in that moment. People knew where to find him far too easily. If he was in a big city, he could blend into the crowds until no one bothered to look sideways at him. No one bothered to meddle.

He opened another beer without looking at Adam and frowned at Ollie. "Some guard dog you are."

"This house only has room for one guard dog."

Him. He transferred his glare to his best friend. "Bite me."

"Wrong again." Adam dropped into the chair next to him and snatched the beer out of his hands. "What the hell were you thinking?"

Word sure as fuck got around fast. Daniel checked his watch. "It's been less than twenty-four hours. How the hell did you find out?"

"You know your cousin. She's got feelers all over this town." Adam motioned with his fingers. "Hope went to Jessica Stroup's after your fight, and Jessica called in Jules as reinforcements." He sent Daniel a significant look. "She also called Mrs. Moore."

Just like that, he was back in that perfectly white room

hearing the woman condemn him with a few well-placed words. *You love your guilt more than you love my daughter.* It merged with the look of betrayal on Hope's face right before she walked out of his life. He rubbed the heel of his hand over his chest. "I don't know where it went wrong." He continued before Adam could tell him he'd fucked up again. "No, that's a lie. It went wrong right around the time I got behind the wheel thirteen years ago."

"For fuck's sake." Adam took a swig of the beer and set it aside. "You're the one who gave me the kick in the ass I needed to stop being a self-fulfilling prophecy. I didn't realize we were going to have to switch roles." Adam reached over and scratched Ollie behind her ear. "That accident fucked us all up. Every single one of us. But let me ask you something—"

"I don't want to hear it." Daniel pushed to his feet, driven by the pent-up tangle of emotions poisoning him. "This shit… I keep hurting her, Adam. It doesn't matter what I do or how I do it, I keep hurting Hope." *What if I hurt our baby the same way?* He scrubbed a hand over his face. "Maybe it'd be best if I just got the hell out of everyone's lives."

He opened his eyes at the sound of clapping and frowned at Adam giving him a standing fucking ovation. "What the hell?"

"Are you done with your pity party?"

"It's not a fucking pity party. It's the truth."

"It's the truth *you're* forcing. Once upon a time, you told me that I just needed to break the cycle. Well, man, look in the mirror." With one last pat of Ollie's head, he started down the porch steps, delivering a parting shot over his shoulder. "But are you really going to be okay with Hope settling down with some other guy and your baby being raised calling someone else Daddy? Because that's what's going to happen if you don't pull your head out of your ass. She might love the shit out of you, but Hope lands on her feet. This time won't be any different. The only choice is whether you're at her side when she does." And then he was gone, climbing into his old truck and taking off down the driveway in a cloud of dust.

"Bastard always did like to make an exit." Daniel dropped back into his chair and stared at the horizon, his thoughts tumbling over themselves and getting nowhere. He wanted to call Adam and rail at him, to tell him that he had no fucking idea what Daniel was going through. But it would be a lie. Out of his two friends, Adam knew better than Quinn. He always had. They both had a vein of guilt that ran deep, though the source wasn't the same. Adam had managed to put his aside.

Daniel wasn't sure he could.

Hope deserved better than him. He'd known it from the time he was a teenager, and that hadn't stopped him from pursuing her then. Hell, it hadn't stopped him the last few weeks, either.

Ollie whined, and he scratched her behind the ears, earning a lick. "It's not that easy."

But the truth of it was, *he* was the only thing standing in his way.

Hope had already proven that she was willing to set aside the past and give him the benefit of the doubt. Her mother might not, but he wasn't trying to have a relationship with her mother. That said, Lisa Moore had some good fucking points. He sighed.

The thing was, he *didn't* totally see his baby as a way to recoup what was lost. Or at least, that wasn't the driving force behind his pushing for Hope to give him another shot. Not when he really thought about it.

The truth was he wanted her in his life and in his bed. He loved her. Fuck, the last few days since they told their families about the pregnancy had been the happiest of his life. He'd actually *wanted* to cook for her, and he'd spent the days looking forward to coming home and finding her there, working or cooking or doing her yoga in the backyard. His shitty little house had started to feel like a home, and it was all because of Hope.

And he'd gone and fucked it up.

Daniel pushed to his feet, startling Ollie. "Sorry, girl." He reached for his phone and then hesitated. A call wasn't going to cut it. He'd let Hope Moore slip out of his life thirteen years ago, and he couldn't live with himself if he did it a second time.

He just had to prove to her that he was all in.

Chapter Seventeen

Hope rolled out of bed at nine, which was the latest her pride would allow her to sleep in. As tempting as it was to hide in bed all day, there were too many things waiting for her attention, not the least being her plan for the future. She combed her hair and put on her brightest sundress, needing to feel in control of at least *that*. She glanced at her phone, hating the little thread of disappointment when the notifications showed no missed calls or texts from Daniel.

He didn't call last time, either.

God, she was so sure she'd moved past all of that. All it took was one fight and she was right back in that dark place, calling and calling and never getting any answer. She wouldn't do that again. She *couldn't*. There was more than herself to think of now, and wallowing in despair couldn't possibly be good for the baby.

That's the only bright spot in this disaster, which is damned ironic.

She pressed her hand to her stomach. "It's just me and you, little bit." Except it *wasn't*. There would be no cutting

Daniel out of her life for good, not when the baby was half him. As much as it made her sick to think about, she had to face him, and soon. They had to hash out some kind of visitation setup before she left town, because she had no intention of setting foot back in Devil's Falls. This town had done enough damage, and it didn't matter if her pain wasn't actually the town's fault.

"Uh, Hope?"

She jumped and then felt guilty for jumping. She was in Jessica's home, after all. It only stood to reason that the woman had come to check on her. "Yeah?"

"I think you're going to want to come see this."

She opened the door and started down the stairs, wondering at how strange her friend sounded. "What's wrong?" When she got no answer, she picked up her pace, though she kept a hand on the railing. The last thing she needed was a tumble, especially when she was already feeling so off balance. She froze at the bottom of the stairs, not quite believing her eyes. "Danny?" She took a step toward him and then stopped, registering that both her parents were on the other side of the living room, and Jessica stood next to them, and all three of them were staring at her and Daniel with varying degrees of expectation.

"Hey, darling." His face didn't give anything away, didn't give *any* indication of why he was here.

Painfully aware they had an audience, she bit her lip. "Maybe we should talk privately." Judging from the way Jessica was practically salivating, anything he said would spread like wildfire through town by lunch. Hope couldn't even blame her. It was just the way things were in this town.

"No, I don't think we should." He moved toward her, and she belatedly registered the flowers in his hands. Daisies. Her favorite.

She took them, not sure what to think. "You remembered."

"I remember everything." He took her hand, and for one breathless moment, she thought he was going to go down on one knee, but Daniel met her gaze, the naked longing in his eyes drawing her in despite herself. He squeezed her hand. "I fucked up. I fucked up when I put myself before us thirteen years ago, and I fucked up again last night by letting the past get a stranglehold on me. I've been so focused on everything that went wrong all that time ago, I forgot to focus on everything going *right*."

"Danny—"

"Let me finish." There was no heat to the words—just quiet strength. "I love you, darling. I've always loved you. The last few days have made me so happy that it scared the shit out of me, and so I went and poked it until it exploded. I was wrong, and I'm so damn sorry."

He was saying everything she'd ever wanted to hear, but she couldn't help waiting for the other shoe to drop. "We tried. We failed. Some things just aren't meant to be."

"You're right." He continued before she could fully process how her heart dropped at his agreement. "Some things aren't. But we aren't some things. A love like ours doesn't come around more than once in a lifetime, and the fact we get a second chance to do it right is miracle enough. I don't deserve a second chance—or third or fourth or whatever number chance we're on now—but I'm here asking for it all the same."

"I don't know what to say." Except she knew what she wanted to say. Hope opened her mouth, forcing the words past her pride demanding she stay silent. "I…I need my own place."

He didn't blink. "I suggest you rent."

"Uh, what?"

"I'm going to marry you, Hope Moore. It can be on your timeline, but it's going to happen." He glanced at her parents, watching the whole thing with unreadable expressions on their faces. "I know I'm not good enough for your daughter, but I'm going to spend the rest of my life working to be." He squeezed her hand again. "I know it'll take time, but the beauty is that we have the rest of our lives to work up to it."

She'd woken up this morning on the very edge of despair, sure that history was repeating itself, and yet here he was, proving her dead wrong. It felt too good to be true.

But, as she looked up at him, she realized it was really happening. "My timeline?"

"I can't promise I won't be pushy from time to time, but I'll respect whatever boundaries you put into place." He reached out and tentatively touched her stomach, as if expecting her to slap his hand away. "Whatever it takes, darling. I'll do it. Just name the price."

Price. For the first time, she understood. That was what he'd never been able to get past before. He was trying—he wouldn't be here if he wasn't—but part of him still expected her to reject him and cut him out of her life. She lifted her chin. "Kiss me."

Daniel's slow grin did a number on her stomach, just like it always had. "You're going easy on me."

"I figure there's a mighty good chance I'll spend the next seven months putting you through the wringer." She covered his hand on her stomach with her own. "Then we have the rest of our lives catering to the whims of this one. And the others."

"Others."

"Danny, you know very well that I want a whole handful of kids."

He smiled so wide, it made her heart leap, because the shadows that never seemed to leave his face were gone. "I guess I'll have to get a few more dogs like Ollie and teach them all to herd so the kids don't run us ragged."

"I guess you will." Was it possible for a person's heart to burst from happiness? Because she was reasonably sure that hers might in that moment as he pulled her into his arms. He paused and looked at her parents again. "While your blessing isn't strictly necessary, I sure would like to have it. On account of the grandbabies."

Hope's dad opened his mouth, but her mom put her hand on his arm and spoke first. "Do right by our daughter, Daniel."

"I plan on it, ma'am."

It wasn't a blessing, strictly speaking, but it was as good as a declaration that her mother would try. Really, that was all anyone could ask for. Hope looked at Daniel, her heartbeat picking up at being so close to him, just like it always did. "I love you."

"I know." He leaned down, stopping just short of actually kissing her. "I love you, too, darling."

Acknowledgments

To God. It's been quite the journey and this year has been more challenging than I could have imagined, but it's all worth it. Thank you.

To Heather Howland. Thank you so much for helping me finagle this series and up my game with Daniel and Hope. Their book wouldn't be what it is without your input.

To Kari Olson. Thank you for pointing me in the direction of Tyler Farr's album, Suffer in Peace. That served as a soundtrack for this book! You know how I adore broken men and their breakup songs!

To the Rabble. Thank you time and time again for your endless support and enthusiasm. You're often the first eyes that see snippets of my books, and your responses never fail to make my day!

To Piper Drake. You've been my sounding board and the person talking me off the ledge for ages now. The last few years wouldn't have been the same without your presence in my life, and I am so damn grateful for you! You're a rockstar!

To Tim. I'm writing this as we're approaching our three

year anniversary. I don't know that anyone has gone through quite as much in such a relatively short period of time. Thank you for being my rock in the storm—and for sometimes being the storm to shove me out of my head. I love you like whoa. Here's to you, babe.

About the Author

New York Times and *USA Today* bestselling author, Katee Robert, learned to tell stories at her grandpa's knee. Her favorites then were the rather epic adventures of The Three Bears, but at age twelve she discovered romance novels and never looked back. Though she dabbled in writing, life got in the way, as it often does, and she spent a few years traveling, living in both Philadelphia and Germany. In between traveling and raising her two wee ones, she had the crazy idea that she'd like to write a book and try to get published.

***If you love sexy romance, one-click these steamy
Brazen releases…***

PLAYING IT COOL
a *Sydney Smoke Rugby* novel by Amy Andrews

Harper Nugent might have a little extra junk in her trunk, but her stepbrother calling her out on it is the last straw… When rugby hottie, Dexter Blake, witnesses the insult, he surprises Harper by asking her out. In front of her dumbass brother. Score! Of course, she knows it's not for reals, but Dex won't take no for an answer. Still the date is better than either expected. So is the next one. And the next. And the heat between them…sizzles their clothes right off. Suddenly, this fake relationship is feeling all too real…

MAKE ME STAY
a *Men of Gold Mountain* novel by Rebecca Brooks

Samantha Kane is about to solidify her father's legacy by developing sleepy Gold Mountain into the most profitable ski resort in the country. There's one man standing in her way though. One very sexy, rugged man. When she shows up to convince Austin Reede to sell, she had no intention of hiding her identity. But what he doesn't know won't hurt him…

HIS BEST MISTAKE

a *Shillings Agency* novel by Diane Alberts

One night with a stranger... Security expert Mark Matthews has loved, and lost, and has no intention of ever loving again—especially not a woman who thrives on her life being in danger. Now, hot, meaningless sex with strangers he had no intention of ever seeing again? That's a whole other story. And it's all life as a single father allows him to enjoy. But when he meets Daisy O'Rourke, the game is on, because she's everything he swore to stay away from. She has bad idea written all over her, but he's in too deep to walk away now...

WORKED UP

a *Made in Jersey* novel by Tessa Bailey

Factory mechanic Duke Crawford just wants to watch SportsCenter in peace. Unfortunately, living with four divorcee sisters doesn't provide much silence, nor does it change his stance on relationships. But when fellow commitment-phobe Samantha Waverly stumbles into his life, he can't deny his protective instincts. The only way out of her family dilemma is to marry Duke—for show, of course. The blistering attraction between them might be hot enough to burn down the world, but their marriage isn't real...or is it?

Serve series

Mistaken By Fate

Betting on Fate

Protecting Fate

Made in the USA
Columbia, SC
03 October 2023

23823059R00102